BY THE BOOK

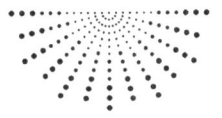

SHERITTA BITIKOFER

Moonstruck Writing

Cover model Chris Mayo by RLS Model Images Photography

ISBN: 978-1-946821-27-0

Ebook ISBN: 978-1-946821-28-7

❀ Created with Vellum

Thank you to my husband who will forever be my romantic inspiration.
Also big thanks to Camp Coyote in Hunstville Texas for teaching me how to ride a horse. I never loved country music until I spent my first amazing summer there.

CHAPTER ONE

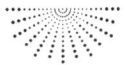

Tara let her fingertips slide over the glossy spines of the paperbacks on the shelf, her eyes skimming over the titles as she slowly ambled down the aisle. The scent of espresso and sugar cookies permeated the Books & Beans Coffee Shop and she could just faintly hear the soft conversation from the café area of the store beyond the bookcases.

Part of her felt as if she were committing adultery against the piles and piles of unread books back at her little apartment on the south side of town. She shouldn't have been looking for a new read when there were so many others waiting at home. It would have taken her more time to run home, make lunch, grab a new book, and hurry back to work. Instead she walked to the little coffee shop-slash-bookstore across the street from her work, for a quick sandwich and a few moments of peace on her lunch break.

Besides, one more book to join her precious family of novels wouldn't hurt. Right? Rachel, the owner of the shop and senior barista, was busy making Tara's usual chai tea latte with a spritz of cinnamon. It was a sweet and spicy pick-me-up to get her through the rest of her day while being stuck behind the counter at the modest dentist office. She loved her job, but sometimes she wished her boss would let them read during the long, slow periods between appointments so she wouldn't be bored. Her escape to the coffee shop was often the high-light of her day, besides going home after five o'clock, of course.

Tara's life wasn't all pathetic. She had her friends, her family, and, of course, her books. Who could ever be bored when there are so many stories to read, so many worlds to immerse in? Romance, mystery, horror, para-normal, fantasy, historical. She loved it all. Which is why picking out a new book could be so hard at times.

The best thing she could do was pick one and just go with it.

Her hand brushed over a spine and she found it wasn't so smooth and pristine as the others. Her gaze trailed back to the worn trade paperback. Thin crease lines cut through the cursive title so much that she could barely read what it said.

Curiosity got the best of her and Tara slipped the book down from its resting place. She found the top edge covered in a thin layer of dust as if it had been sitting there undisturbed for months.

It certainly was old. The cover art reminded her of the trashy romance novels her mother used to read. The kind that looked as if it were painted or drawn, rather than photographed and spritzed up with Photoshop. She gazed upon the image of a man, his button-down shirt undone to reveal his rock-hard chest and abs beneath. His piercing blue eyes stared back at her, his slightly wavy black hair tucked underneath a dashing cowboy hat.

With a lasso in one hand and a cattle brand in the other, he looked the part of a rough and tumble ranch hand. In the distance, a brilliant golden sunset blazed across the sky with a girl riding a white horse on the horizon. With her long, dark hair flowing in the fictional breeze, no one would second guess that she was the one the cowboy was going to claim through the course of the story.

The title scrawled out in an elegant font

read, "Texas Bounty". Tara tried to hold in a laugh as she tossed her dark hair over her shoulder. She had never heard of the title or the author before. A quick peek at the back description, however, set her heart racing. Packed with romance, intrigue, and danger, it looked like just her kind of book.

Oddly enough, there was no price on the cover. Rachel normally kept her shelves stocked with the newest best sellers and some titles from local authors, but she had never seen a used book like this floating around. Maybe someone came and dropped it off without thinking.

"Tara! Your tea's ready!" Rachel called from the coffee counter near the front of the store.

She hurried to the café section of the shop with her intended purchase. On the counter sat her cup of steaming tea and the turkey bacon sandwich she had also ordered. Rachel grinned when she saw Tara walk up with the book.

"Don't you have enough?" she teased.

Tara only smiled. "One can never have enough books," she said as she slid the novel across the counter. "I don't see a price on this one, though."

Rachel's dark eyes took in the cover and then picked it up to check the inside. "I don't either. I don't recognize it. There isn't even a barcode on the back."

"That means it's free then, right?" Tara asked before taking the first sip of her tea. Perfection.

Rachel shrugged her slender shoulders and brush back a strand of blonde hair that escaped from her messy bun. "I guess so. Happy early birthday."

She laughed as the owner handed the book back to her. "Four months early. Fantastic!"

The girls giggled to one another and Tara balanced her sandwich plate on top of the book as she made her way to one of the little round tables just big enough for her and maybe one other person. With the way her long legs occupied most of the space beneath the table, it would have been a tight fit.

She settled herself in the seat, crossed her legs and checked her phone to make sure she had enough time to spare on her lunch break. Twenty-five minutes to go. Plenty of time to find out if she would like her new book.

It even smelled like a new book, despite the obvious evidence of dog-eared corners and slightly wrinkled edges of the old style cover. A quick peek to the inside told her that it was published on her birth year, twenty-five years ago. Suddenly, the book seemed a little more special.

She took another sip of her tea and with the book propped open in one hand, she began eating her sandwich in the other. Minutes ticked by as she stepped into the world of a contemporary small town in Texas. For the most part, it sounded just like her hometown of Brooksdale. One main thoroughfare, one big shopping center, and dozens of mom-and-pop stores that lined the main street of the town. She was born and raised in Brooksdale, just a few hours southwest of Houston and nestled in the heart of prime Texas ranchland that was alternatively used for raising cattle or oil drilling. The people were friendly, though perhaps a little old fashioned.

Then, she was introduced to the heroine. Independent and slightly awkward, Tara immediately identified with her. Just from the little interactions that were described between Trish and some of the other characters, she seemed smart, funny, and a lover of books just like Tara. She wondered if her boss would buy the lie that she had lost track of time on her lunch break. Already hooked, she knew she could get lost between these covers all too easily.

Within the first two chapters, the hero

appeared, the man showcased so spectacularly on the cover. Tara held the sandwich over her plate, the juices from the meat dripping into a puddle on the Styrofoam as she felt completely enraptured. The hero and heroine were about to meet in a little coffee shop, just like the one she was currently sitting in.

She hardly noticed when the front door dinged and slowly swung open to admit a new customer. Tara glanced up briefly as the tall man walked past her toward the counter, but she didn't bother to take a good look. His heavy boots tapped against the tile floor and faded jeans hung loose around his hips. She did a double-take when his scent wafted to her, following just a second and a half after he had already passed by. He smelled just like the great outdoors, but there was a subtle hint of a strong cologne that made her mouth water.

Tara turned in her chair and let her hazel eyes roam over his broad shoulders and the way his short-sleeve shirt hugged his thick, powerful muscles. The bottom hem of his jeans were speckled with dry mud so she knew he must have been a blue-collar worker. They were a dime a dozen in this town, not too uncommon, but nothing about this guy looked ordinary.

His arms were tanned, more tan than hers anyway, as well as the back of his neck. Black, slightly wavy hair crowned his head, but was cut short, probably so it wouldn't be too hard to tame back in the morning.

Her eyes wandered down his back, not feeling the least bit shameful for the way she checked him out. She could only hope that his face was just as pretty as his body. Now she was kicking herself for not having paid closer attention when he first walked in. She could see the way Rachel appraised him in a not-so-subtle way that told Tara all she needed to know.

"Coffee. Black."

Even his voice was sexy. Deep, rumbling, the kind that Tara imagined when reading a steamy romance. To hear the voice in real life gave her pleasant shivers.

He paid for his drink and stood off to the side to wait. Tara was dumbstruck by the face that briefly turned in her direction. She quickly swiveled back around and tried to act like she hadn't just been staring. Yet, she couldn't get his piercing blue eyes or scruffy, handsome features out of her mind.

Slowly, she flipped over the cover on her book and saw that same face looking back at her with such hungry, lustful intent. Her heart hammered in her throat. There was no way this guy was the model for the book cover. It was published twenty-five years ago and this guy looked to be just about as old as her. If the style of the cover wasn't so dated, she might have suspected that this was a newer edition with a new cover.

It had to be a coincidence. Either way, Tara lowered her book a little closer to the tabletop so he wouldn't catch a glimpse of his cowboy lookalike. The only thing this stranger was missing was the lasso, the brand, and the sexy female with a horse in the background.

Tara went back to reading, though every fiber of her being wanted to turn around and ogle at him a little more before he left with his coffee. A few paragraphs further, though, she noticed a few more coincidences.

In the scene where Trish meets her intended lover, the cowboy's pant legs were also muddied, and he ordered black coffee. Not only that, but Trish, the heroine, was doing exactly what Tara was doing, right down to hiding the cover and eating a turkey bacon sandwich. What was going on?

Her hands began to tremble and she placed her half-eaten sandwich on the plate to risk flipping a few pages ahead.

They were blank.

Tara had seen printing accidents where a page or two were left completely empty, but this wasn't the same thing. The rest of the chapter was just gone. In fact, the further she skimmed, she found the rest of the book to be completely blank too. But this wasn't a printing mistake. The author's name, page number, and page title were still featured on the top page. It was as if the rest of the story just wasn't there for her to read.

If it weren't so quiet and peaceful in the café, she would have let out a loud expletive that would certainly get everyone's attention.

Tara closed the book and sat back in her chair, staring at the back cover with her brows pinched together. Something wasn't right here, but once again, the same curiosity that got her to pull the book down from the shelf in the first place, prompted her to open it up once more. The story was too good to pass up, no matter how eerily similar it was to what was going on in this very moment.

She found where she had left off and turned the page to continue. This time, the page wasn't blank. It was filled with text and from what she briefly saw, there was a ton of dialogue. The two characters were about to meet for sure, but Tara was more interested in testing the book again. She flipped a few more pages, but they were blank just as before. The text was filling itself in the more she read.

It was like the book knew what she had read so far. Or maybe, it wasn't following her as much as it was following the natural flow of time. Tara swallowed hard and looked back to the guy waiting at the counter. He wasn't talking with Rachel, or anyone else for that matter. Instead of his eyes being glued to a smart phone, they wandered around the café and bookstore, as if memorizing every detail, just as the book said he was.

This was crazy. A book couldn't predict the future and neither could Tara. This guy couldn't be the cowboy on the front cover and there was no way she was Trish from the story. It wasn't possible. But she kept reading and watching, looking over her shoulder until the man's eyes fell on her table and lingered there a little too long.

Tara slunk in her chair and uncrossed her legs to squeeze her knees together, trying to make herself as small and inconspicuous as possible. She turned her attention solely on the book. In the story, the main hero walked up to the heroine's table and she accidentally spilled her drink all over his jeans. Tara wasn't clumsy, another strike against the possibility that she was Trish.

"Hey," the deep voice rumbled beside her.

Tara jerked and just like in the story, her

arm knocked straight into her chai latte and it went tumbling over the edge of the table. The lid popped off as it crashed to the floor. Hot tea poured onto the tile and a good portion of it darkened the fabric on the stranger's jeans.

She gasped and grabbed for the stack of napkins Rachel had given with the sandwich. The book dropped closed and she lost her spot, but that was the farthest thing from Tara's mind.

"Oh my God, I'm so sorry!" she cried. Rachel and the few other people who were in the café turned to watch her begin frantically patting up the hot tea that had spilled on the surface of the table.

The stranger only laughed and took a few napkins to help mop up the mess on the floor. "It's all right," he said. "These are my work jeans anyway. They've gotten dirtier."

That was exactly what the cowboy in the story said, right down to the laugh and everything.

Tara's cheeks blushed a deep red. "I'm normally not a klutz, I swear."

Her gaze finally lifted and she wondered if she would ever breathe again. Up close, this guy wasn't just a hottie. He might have been the sexiest man she had ever seen, and that was saying something since she had stared at tons of romance novel covers in her time. None of them could compare to him. Even the guy on the mysterious fortune-telling book in front of her couldn't do the real-life thing justice.

He gave her a gorgeous smile and she took a breath. "It's fine, really," he assured, then pointed to something on her table. Oh god, what if he saw the book cover and was about to ask her questions that she couldn't answer? "I was just looking at that little table tent and wanted to get a better look."

Tara looked and saw the tiny, folded advertisement. She remembered when Rachel set them out almost a week ago to help promote the carnival that was coming to town. Tonight was the opening night according to the information on the card.

She quickly reached out and handed the table tent to the stranger as she wiped up the rest of the spilled tea.

"The carnival's pretty fun," she said as she set her to-go cup upright. "I used to go a lot as a kid when my parents took me."

She looked up and saw the guy nod in approval. "I'm looking for something for me and my niece to do. Her dad's going to be busy with work so I'm taking her out."

Tara wanted to swoon. Sexy and a family man. "Does she like to go to the carnival?" she asked, feeling a bit silly for the question. What kid didn't love to go on rides, pet the goats, and get sick off of cotton candy?

"I'm not sure. I know her and her mother used to go out and do fun things like this."

Used to. Tara wanted to pry, but she didn't even know his name. Asking personal family information would have been a little creepy.

She wadded up the soiled napkins and stuffed them down her now empty tea cup. "I'm sure she'll love it, then. I always like the Ferris wheel and the shooting gallery games."

Now she was over sharing.

He smiled to her and put the ad back on the table, leaning over her a bit in order to do it. Tara took a deep whiff and hoped he didn't notice. Damn, he smelled good.

"Are you going tonight?" he asked, pulling her out of her fantasy for a moment.

Tara shrugged. "Probably not. I tend to spend my evenings at home nowadays."

There she went again, oversharing and making herself look like a pitiful, lonely single woman.

He didn't seem to notice – either that or he didn't mind at all – because he went on to say, "Well, maybe you can make an exception tonight. If Dixie's never been to a fair, I'm not going to know the first thing about what she'll like or not like. Maybe you could come with us and show us all the fun stuff to do. I remember going to fairs when I was a kid, but what I like may not be what she likes."

If Tara didn't have a good handle on herself, she might have let her jaw drop in disbelief. Was this guy asking her out? No, he wasn't asking her out on a date. He was asking if she could come along and show his niece a good time. This had nothing to do with her. She had to keep that in mind or she would blow it way out of proportion, just like she did everything else.

"Sure," she replied with a grin. "That'd be fun... My name's Tara, by the way." She offered out her hand.

"Beau," he introduced, wrapping his fingers around hers in a firm, but friendly handshake. Something in her made her grip his hand a little harder and his brows shot up. "Nice handshake."

Oh God, what if he was turned off by a girl that asserted herself? Tara let go quickly and let her hand drop to her lap so he wouldn't see how badly she was shaking. "Sorry. Bad habit."

"No," he laughed. "I like it."

Tara wanted to breathe a sigh of relief, but she refrained and kept her wits about her. As if that were even possible when Beau was looking at her.

"So, the doors open up at four," he continued. "We can meet you at the ticket booth at five."

She winced. "I actually work until five and then I have to grab dinner. Would six be okay?" That little nagging voice in the back of her head berated her for trying to negotiate terms with Beau. She was the one doing them the service, not the other way around. Maybe she could try and find a way to get off early.

Beau slipped his hands into his front jean pockets and she couldn't help but notice the way his muscles moved so erotically beneath his skin. "That'll work. Do you think the food at the carnival is safe to eat? I've been to some where the food tasted good, but you'd regret it the next morning."

Tara giggled, though joking over food poisoning wasn't exactly supposed to be funny. "I never got sick from eating the carnival food around here, so she should be safe. In that case, we could make it five-thirty. I can just grab some food with y'all."

He gave a nod, as if the deal was sealed. "Great. I'll see you then, Tara. It was nice to meet you."

"Nice to meet you too," she said through

possibly the biggest grin in the history of grins. "Looking forward to it."

He turned away and met Rachel at the counter to take his coffee. As he walked out the door, she saw him glance at her over his shoulder. Beau smiled and gave a little wave before leaving, but Tara was nearly frozen with that goofy smile still plastered on her face.

This was insane. She was going on a date with the hottest guy she had ever met, and it was all about his niece having a good time. Not them. That was new, yet oddly endearing.

When her world came back into focus, Tara snatched up the book and peeled through the pages to find where she had left off. Sure enough, the following few pages that were once blank were now filled. Every piece of dialogue, every action and internal thought she had, was exactly mirrored in the story.

Even more insane than her date with Beau, was the existence of this book. Could it tell the future? Or was she secretly dictating what needed to be in the book based on what was happening in her life? Would she be able to read Beau's point of view? By the way the pages hadn't manifested farther than the moment he walked out, she knew there must have been a limit somewhere. It wasn't going to tell her anything beyond the present, or beyond what she was experiencing.

The alarm went off on her phone, telling her it was time to return to reality. She needed to run across the street, back to the desk job she so desperately wanted to throw out the window. Maybe the heroine in the book will get a new job by the end of the story. One thing's for sure, the other books on her to-be-read list would have to wait until this new drama played out.

CHAPTER TWO

"You didn't even get his last name?" Rebecca whispered. Tara had just finished telling her coworker all about Beau and the pure fairytale introduction they had at the coffee shop. What else were they supposed to do, sitting at the front desk with no other scheduled appointments for another couple of hours?

Tara leaned her head in her hand and sighed. "No. In the rush of everything, I didn't even think about it."

Rebecca flipped her blonde hair over her shoulder. "How else are you going to stalk him on Facebook if you don't have a last name?" She immediately pulled out her phone to begin the search. "Did he mention anything else besides that he's helping out his brother and niece?"

"Not really. His niece's name is Dixie, but that won't help you find him." Tara thought for a moment. "Well, he looked like he had been working outside. His clothes were a little muddy."

Rebecca stopped and turned to look at Tara with her brows arched. "Dixie Bremor?"

"He never mentioned a last name," Tara groaned and reached over to retrieve her new book from her purse. For the hundredth time since lunch, she quickly flipped through the pages. Not only was she checking for any hints as to Beau's identity, but also if there were any new pages to read. Nothing.

She heard a few hasty taps on Rebecca's phone and then her friend angled the screen. "Is this him?"

Tara peeked over and saw the familiar handsome face staring back at her, his eyes covered by a pair of sunglasses and a hefty fish dangling from a line in his hand. It didn't surprise her that he would be a man of the outdoors. "Yeah, that's him," she said excitedly, dropping her book in favor of Rebecca's phone. She started scrolling through his profile, careful not to let her fingers slide over the cracked glass of the screen. Rebecca was never careful with her stuff. Ever since they met in elementary school, Rebecca was always dropping toys, spilling drinks, or losing her stuff. Little had changed.

When Tara confirmed that the guy in the picture was the same guy she had met at the coffee shop, Rebecca flipped. "This must be Daniel Bremor's brother!" she exclaimed.

Tara's face wrinkled with confusion. She remembered Daniel from high school. He was the hottest quarterback on the football team and had even gotten a scholarship to go to Sam Houston State University after he graduated. Everyone had a crush on him, including Rebecca.

She knew Daniel had moved back after college to take over the family ranch. He married, of course, and had a kid, Dixie. "I didn't know Daniel had a brother."

Rebecca lightly smacked the back of her hand on Tara's arm. "Sure he did. We had chemistry with him in our Junior year."

Tara searched her memory, but couldn't find that handsome face sitting in the rows of lab tables. She would have certainly remembered a face like his. She slowly shook her head, wondering if Rebecca was thinking of someone else.

She shrugged. "Okay, so he really beefed out," Rebecca corrected. "He sat way in the back, always had the right answers..."

It was as if the lightbulb had gone off over her head. "The kid who was really good with the ignitor things for the burners?"

Rebecca snapped her finger. "That's the guy."

She looked down to his picture again, this time her eyes went wide. "Wow, he did beef up. He doesn't even look like the same kid."

"I bet Beau's in town because of the accident."

Tara snapped a look at her friend. "Accident?"

"Dixie's mom," she said. "She got in a bad car wreck driving Dixie to school one morning. Dixie was fine, but her mom didn't make it."

Tara lowered her hands to let them rest on the countertop as her chest ached. "That's Beau's niece? I heard about that. Poor thing."

Every time Dixie came in, she skipped right up to the counter, her black curls bouncing all the way, hair just like Beau's. Unlike some of the other kids that came through those doors, she wasn't afraid of the dentist. In fact, she looked forward to it, because her dad always promised to get her ice cream if she behaved for the doctor. That must have been why she needed to have a filling not too long ago.

It all made sense now. Beau must have

been in town so he could help Daniel and Dixie get back on their feet after the accident. She didn't know what it was like to lose a parent. Both of hers were still alive and well in the next town over and visited on occasion. Her mother had been a lifeline for her during her teenage years and to think that Dixie, as well as millions of girls like her, would grow up without a mother nearly broke her heart.

Beau's dedication and loyalty to his family made Tara ache to know him even more. Better yet, she wanted to find out how he made such a turnaround from the smart chemistry kid who sat in the back of class to this hunky cowboy with canons for arms. What did he do after high school? Did he recognize her? Did he think she was rude for not recognizing him right off the bat?

She looked back to his profile and saw the one thing she had been looking for. His relationship status. Single. It was a relief, but how relieved could she be to know that the only reason he had come into her life so suddenly was because of a devastating tragedy?

Tara couldn't be glad that Dixie had lost her mother. But she could be glad that Beau cared enough about his family to leave wherever it was he came from and move to Brooksdale to be closer to them. At least she wouldn't go to the carnival tonight and be blind-sided when she saw Dixie standing next to the tall, sexy, compassionate cowboy. The cowboy who had stolen her heart the moment those blue eyes looked at her.

"Are you still going to the carnival tonight?" Rebecca asked, crossing her arms over the counter.

Tara started flipping through his photos, looking for any sign that Beau might have been with a girl recently. So far, all of his photos were taken by himself or with friends. She saw a few holiday pictures that featured Dixie, Daniel, and his late wife. "Of course I am," she replied. "Why wouldn't I?"

"Just the drama. I mean, I haven't seen Dixie since before the accident. I don't know how she's been handling it."

Tara shrugged. "She must be doing fine, considering that Beau wants to take her to the carnival. If she wasn't ready to go out and have a fun time, he wouldn't have considered it."

Rebecca peeked over at the phone and moaned at the one picture of Beau, shirtless and by a creek, about to jump in. By the other people in the water, it must have been from a time when he and a bunch of his friends decided to cool off during the summer. He sure was sexy in his navy blue swim trunks that hung low on his hips.

"Isn't that yummy," Rebecca remarked. "If you can snag him up, I'd do it. Kind of a real life Cinderella story, isn't it?"

Tara bit her lip and thought about the book again. She wasn't even a quarter of the way through. There was plenty more left to this story, but how much more? She still wasn't convinced that she was the girl on the horse in the background of the cover. If she was, this was going to be some whirlwind romance. Closing time couldn't come soon enough.

"ARE YOU COLD, BABY?" Beau asked Dixie, looking down to her as she aimlessly wandered in circles across the patch of grass next to the carnival entrance. Behind them, colorful lights flickered in the darkness and the squeals of giddy children echoed in the evening air.

"For the tenth time, I'm fine," Dixie retorted after she groaned. "And before you ask again, no I'm not thirsty. But I am hungry. How much longer do we have to wait?"

Beau had to admit that they had arrived pretty early. He was perhaps a little too eager to see Tara again, for which he chided himself. He shouldn't have been so drawn to her like this. Not after spending years apart.

The moment he saw her in the coffee shop, Beau immediately recognized her from high school. His disappointment equaled his surprise when she didn't seem to recognize him in return. He couldn't blame her. He wasn't all that impressive in high school. It wasn't until the summer after his senior year when he went to engineering school that he started to bulk up. The minute that happened, girls were falling at his feet. But none were like Tara.

He had never forgotten her or her beautiful hazel eyes. In school, he was afflicted with an enormous crush on the dark-haired girl that sat in the second row of their chemistry class. If he had any guts back then, he would have asked her out. It was too bad he didn't, otherwise things could have been different for them now. She was still beautiful, but he was sorely unavailable for romance.

He had to remind himself that he didn't invite Tara to come to the carnival so he could personally spend time with her or catch up on old memories. Well, maybe that had a little to do with it. But the impatient eight-year-old had a heavier influence in his decision to extend the invitation. Her dad who was too busy with business tonight to come along. Instead of arguing with his brother, Beau let Daniel further distance himself from Dixie one more time.

He pulled out his phone and checked the time. "Not much longer. We'll grab some food as soon as she gets here."

Dixie kicked at a loose leaf. "Where did you meet her again?"

Beau saw the top button of her jacket was undone and squatted down to fasten it. "At the coffee shop across the street from the dentist."

The little girl held still, though she rolled her eyes. Dixie might have hated wearing so many layers, but Beau wasn't going to risk her catching a cold. The weather station said the temperature would drop again that evening, not too unusual for early February weather.

"Are you going to marry her?" she asked a little too loudly as a family of four rushed by to stand in line at the ticket booth.

"Nope," Beau replied with utter confidence. If everything went well, he wouldn't be the one getting married, but he wouldn't mind being the best man for his brother again. He'd be losing Tara to a worthy guy, even if he was always the one to land the girl instead of Beau.

"Then why are we waiting on her?" she whined and stamped her foot.

Beau snapped his fingers and pointed at her

nose. Immediately, she straightened up and looked rather sheepish. Daniel had let her get away with far too much, but Beau was going to help change all that. He loved his niece like any other uncle would, but he wasn't going to spoil her. Not like Daniel did.

He stood up and kept her still with his hand on her shoulder. "Because I want you to meet her."

Dixie went quiet, even though he knew she was constantly looking toward the big rides and brightly lit game booths.

Beau took a deep breath to soothe out the jitters he felt deep in his stomach. Yeah, Tara had really messed him up with those hazel eyes and the way she flipped back her long brown hair when she sat up straight after cleaning the tea off the floor. Her clumsiness didn't bother him. It was the way she had stolen the very breath from his lungs when she smiled. That same smile he drooled over as a junior in high school.

He hadn't been so star-struck by a girl like that in such a long time that he forgot what it was like to be totally taken by someone before he even knew their name. Worst part was that he had to keep his heart on a tight leash or this plan would never work.

He finally spotted Tara as she walked out

of the parking lot and right up to them with a big grin. He loved the way her jeans hugged her long legs and how the knitted shawl hung around her elegant shoulders. Even in the fading light of the evening, she was gorgeous. He felt a little over dressed in his black button-down shirt and gray scarf. His boots – now clean and free of the muck and mud from the horse stables – kept his outfit a little less formal.

"Hey," Tara greeted in a voice that denoted her nervousness, though her face didn't betray a bit of that anxiety.

Dixie perked up. "You work at the dentist, don't you?"

Beau squeezed her shoulder. "No, Dixie. I said I met her at the –"

"I know what you said, but she works at the dentist. Don't you?"

Tara's grin broadened. "Yes, I do. You and your dad come in sometimes. How's that filling doing?"

Dixie, being the goof that she was, stuck her finger in her mouth and reach back as if she were checking that her tooth was still there. Then, she shrugged and smiled. "It's all right," she said. She looked up to her uncle, waiting for him to say something too.

"I didn't know you two had met before."

Tara adjusted the shoulder strap of her

purse. "I didn't realize it either until just now. Small town, huh?"

Beau smiled and nodded. "I guess it is."

"Can we get food now?" Dixie asked, still impetuous.

"Did I keep you waiting long?" Tara's smile faded a bit.

"No, no. We just got here a little early."

Beau escorted the girls to the ticket booth and paid for their admission. Dixie would have taken off like a shot if Beau hadn't still had his hand propped on her shoulder. She had a bad habit of running off into crowds and she was way too old to wear one of those toddler leash packs he saw some mothers use.

Tara took the lead and walked them straight towards the concession stand that already had a long line forming. The aroma of deep-fried goodness drifted out from the windows on the food truck and Beau's stomach rumbled in response. Apparently Dixie wasn't the only one hungry.

"I can't see the menu," Dixie complained as she hopped on her tiptoes to see over the heads of the other adults.

Without being asked, Beau lifted her up and braced her against his chest so she was a few feet above the crowd. She wasn't nearly as heavy as a calf, so he could probably hold her like that for a while before his arms would tire.

"You use her for working out?" Tara joked as she stepped a little closer to them. The faint, flowery scent of her perfume made his head spin in a good way.

He saw the way she seemed to appraise the strain of his arm muscles against the fabric of his sleeves. His core tightened under her hungry gaze and he hated the way his pants fit a little snug around his crotch all of the sudden. She still had an effect on him after all these years.

"No, but working on a ranch can be an advantage sometimes."

"You work on Daniel's ranch?" she asked as they took another step forward to keep up with the line. The question shouldn't have caught him off guard. If she knew Dixie, then she should have known Daniel. It was a small town, after all, and they did all go to high school together. Daniel was the popular one, so it made sense that she would have known who his brother was. It only pained Beau further that she didn't seem to remember him.

"I know what I want," Dixie exclaimed and Beau let her down to stand on her own feet again.

"For now, I do," Beau answered. "He's

having to take care of the books now, so I'm taking his place in the field. Before I moved to Brooksdale, I worked on an oil rig."

Tara nodded, but thankfully didn't ask why Daniel had to stay cooped up inside now, sitting in front of his laptop to try and juggle the finances and records. Maybe Tara already knew. Not only did Dixie lose her mother, but Daniel lost his business partner. Beau was sure there were days that Daniel wished he could have been out with the guys, taking care of the livestock and getting his hands dirty. He would have preferred it over the perpetual headache he earned after staring at numbers and account figures for half of the day.

They came to the front of the line and, once again, Beau paid for the three of them.

"You don't have to do that," Tara remarked with a coy look that thankfully went unnoticed by Dixie.

"But I want to." If he wasn't careful, he would have returned that look with one of his own. It was proving incredibly difficult not to flirt with her.

She let the matter go at that and thanked him anyway. All three ordered chilidogs, each customized with different toppings. Dixie had to be the odd one and get relish as well as chili.

"How does that taste?" Tara asked her when they finally sat down with their meals.

"Awesome!" the eight-year-old exclaimed with her mouth full and a dribble of chili sauce leaking at the corners of her lips.

Beau grabbed a napkin and wiped at her mouth, much to Dixie's displeasure.

"Can I try?" Tara asked.

Brows shot up in surprise as Tara went to fetch a fork from the food truck. She came back and with Dixie's permission, scooped some of the weird condiment mix off of her hot dog and plopped it on her own. Beau watched her take a bite and make a face as if to say, "Not so bad."

"Well?" Dixie said, a grin splitting her face.

Tara nodded. "Pretty good. Thanks for the suggestion."

He didn't even have the courage to try some of Dixie's odd food combinations sometimes. Pizza and ranch was a stretch for him. If she could tolerate his niece's quirky interests, she had to be a keeper. It certainly mattered if Daniel liked her, but if Dixie didn't care for her at all, it was a deal breaker.

"So, you went to work on an oil rig after high school?" she questioned before taking a bite of her chilidog.

Beau found it hard to swallow, attempting to empty his mouth to speak. "I was wondering if you recognized me at all, but I wasn't going to ask."

Tara colored a bit. "I'll admit that I didn't recognize you at first, but I realized it later. Did you know who I was when we met in the coffee shop?"

As expected, Dixie immediately perked up and looked from Beau to Tara, her curls dancing around her ears with the motion. Thankfully, she said nothing yet.

"I did," he replied. "You haven't changed since eleventh grade chemistry."

Saying too much might have given himself away in that moment. Remembering such a fine detail might have come out as creepy or obsessive. Granted, Beau had been obsessed with her for a time. It was torture to leave Brooksdale, knowing that he might never have a chance with her again. Throughout his final years at Brooksdale High, he had never had a crush on anyone else but Tara. When he came back to town, he thought she would have moved away or it would have been unlikely that they would meet again in public.

If only they had met under other circumstances.

Tara wiped her mouth on a napkin and smiled. "I can't say the same for you. You definitely... Well, you know." She made a gesture toward his chest and torso from across the table and he couldn't help but chuckle at her loss of words.

"Yeah, I guess I did. And here I thought you never noticed me."

She shrugged. "I notice a lot of things. Remembering them is the hard part."

He wasn't sure whether to take that as a sort of consolation, that he wasn't the only thing she was likely to forget, or an insult that he wasn't memorable enough to stick in her mind as she did for him.

"But to answer your question, yes, I went to work on the oil rig after high school."

Instead of asking why he had moved away, Tara proceeded to ask about the finer details of his job.

He answered each question with complete modesty, though he could tell that she was hanging off his every word, even when he went into the complicated workings of what he did on his old job.

Dixie soon lost interest in their conversation and began to look all around at the distracting carnival lights and sounds.

"I see Brooksdale hasn't changed a lot," he said, hoping to divert from himself for a moment. He was much more interested in hearing about her life after high school. Did she go to college? Why was she working at a dentist office when he knew her passion was for books and reading. She should have been working at the library, or maybe teaching English at the school.

Tara tossed her napkin into the little box her chilidog had been served in. "No, it hasn't. I mean, some of the stores on Main Street have changed owners and we've gotten a couple more fast food places, but other than that, it's the same ole' little town in the middle of nowhere."

She said it all with such a smile that no one would have to guess why she never left Brooksdale. She loved it here. It held no painful memories like it did for Beau.

He nodded and folded his arms over the picnic tabletop they sat at. "So what have you been up to? Since high school, I mean."

Tara shrugged nonchalantly. "Not much. I never went to college. I got plenty of scholarships, but they weren't enough to pay for the tuition I wanted and my parents couldn't pay the difference. They're living in Morrisville now, about an hour away. They moved there when my mawmaw got sick, but I stayed here. I've been working at the dentist for a few years now and I like it pretty well."

There was hope in the way she never

mentioned a boyfriend or marriage. That meant she was single, which lined her up nicely for his plan. God, how he wished he didn't love his brother and niece so much. How he wished he wasn't so selfless sometimes. By the way Tara looked at him now, he could have probably asked her to go with him behind the shooting gallery for a little making out and she'd skip with him all the way. But he couldn't have her.

"I'm sorry to hear your mawmaw got sick," was all he could say.

Tara didn't go into too many details about her grandmother's illness and, if it wasn't for the way Dixie impatiently grabbed for their empty plates to dispose of them, they might have kept talking all night.

His niece tossed their wrappers away into the metal barrel that was already swarming with flies, and came running back to wait for the two grownups to stand. Tara gave him a look that promised they could talk more later, and he sincerely hoped that they would.

"Let's go on the spiny ride!" Dixie offered, and she almost ran out into the crowd again.

Tara was the one to hold her back with a firm hand grabbing her arm. It wasn't every day Beau met someone quicker than him. "Word of advice, kid," she said teasingly. "You just ate.

Don't go on any of those kind of rides for at least an hour."

Dixie looked a little dejected, but gave in. "What do you want to do then?"

Beau, playing the chaperone, hung back as the two ladies walked side by side toward a ring-toss booth. They talked softly and giggled as he slipped his hands into his pockets, enjoying the sight.

Everything was going great. Dixie already seemed to like Tara. Likewise, Tara seemed to get along well with Dixie. Perhaps working at a dentist office had something to do with that. She'd had to deal with nervous kids all the time and help to make them feel comfortable, while the doctor probed at their gums.

Occasionally, Tara glanced over her shoulder to take a peek at Beau and caught him staring with a goofy grin. He didn't even bother looking away, but neither did he feel any shame for admiring Tara. He couldn't explain exactly what it was that drew him to her in the first place, not in school and not now. It wasn't just that she was pretty. He had dated pretty girls before, but they had all been fairly shallow and wanting in the personality department. None could compare to Tara. He had always known her to be smart, witty, and exceedingly kind to everyone, even in school.

Booth after booth, they played games and won prizes for Beau to carry. He sponsored their fun and was glad that he had taken out a couple hundred from the ATM before they came over.

The night continued on that way until they decided to take on some of the rides. Beau left Tara in charge of Dixie for a moment while he went to deposit their earnings from the games. Three stuffed bears, one porcelain elephant, an inflatable superhero toy, and a giant purple monkey that Tara won for Dixie at the shooting gallery. It was a good thing that Beau wasn't a prideful guy, otherwise he might have been intimidated by a woman who could handle a rifle as well as he could.

When he came back, it took a moment for him to find the two. He hastened through the crowd, trying to guess which ride they would have gone on first. Then, he heard his name being screamed from the cyclone ride Dixie had wanted to go on from the very beginning.

Still playing the part of the spectator to their night of fun, Beau leaned against the barrier fence and watched them whirl and spin with their hands in the air.

He wished he could have been on the ride with them, to sit so close to Tara that their thighs were touching. This whole outing was his plan to get Dixie out of the house, but it had morphed into something of a match-making game. If Tara could win Dixie over, the next logical step was to get Daniel on board with dating again. They needed a woman around the house and with his brother neck-deep in business work, he wasn't going to get out and find himself a new wife.

He knew plenty of guys who could bounce back from losing their wives, but Daniel was not one of them. He was going to fester in his grief if he couldn't find another companion. His little brother could never be alone for too long. Hell, he and Erica got married just six months after knowing one another. It might take Daniel a little longer than six months this time around, but if he could learn to love a woman like Tara as quickly as Beau had, their problems would be solved.

Question was, how would Dixie feel about having a stepmom?

By the huge smile on her gleeful face, Beau suspected that the little girl wouldn't mind hanging out with Tara more often. Hell, Beau wouldn't mind either. Actually, he wished that he could sneak in some alone time with her, but the way his heart was behaving, that was totally out of the question. The last thing he needed was to fall for Tara all over again.

The girls exited the ride and came up to him, breathless and wearing the biggest smiles he had ever seen.

"That was so much fun!" Dixie cried as she tugged on his jacket sleeve. "I want to go again!"

Beau glanced to Tara behind the girl, who made a slicing motion with her neck and covered her stomach. He understood and took Dixie's hand. "Come on, I'll go on the ride with you this time."

Dixie jumped for joy.

THE REST of the night was pure magic. Tara didn't know what she enjoyed more, getting to hang out with such an amazing girl as Dixie, or being so close to Beau and those smoldering eyes that fell on her every now and again. He took her breath away so much, she was sure sometimes she would lose control of herself and embrace him right then and there. Whether it was taking aim at a target at the shooting gallery or standing in line for the Ferris Wheel, he lingered so close that she could smell his cologne wafting off him. Enrapturing.

When it was getting close to Dixie's bedtime, they wrapped up their evening with one more go through the spinning ride. Making their way out to the parking lot, Tara couldn't remember having such a great time on a date that wasn't really a date. She wasn't so silly to think that this evening had anything to do with her and Beau, which was why she focused her attention and energy on making sure Dixie had a great time.

She hadn't forgotten what Rebecca told her and, after the rough time Dixie's family must have had, a distracting night at the carnival was just what the little girl needed. And she was so glad that Beau understood that.

"Want me to get your prizes out of the truck?" Beau asked, jerking his thumb toward the opposite end of the parking lot. Tara had parked on the other side.

"No," she replied. "Let Dixie have those. I don't have room in my apartment for all those stuffed animals."

"Really?" Dixie cried, tearing her attention away from the big moon above to skip over to Tara. "Thank you!"

Her skinny arms wrapped around Tara's midsection and squeezed so hard that she thought that chilidog from earlier would finally make an exit. She hugged the girl back and held in the nausea. She had never liked the big spinning rides, or the height of the Ferris wheel, but she wasn't going to let either of them know that. Again, this night wasn't about her.

Dixie finished her hug and hurried toward the red pickup truck, leaving Beau and Tara alone for the first time all evening.

"I had a great time," she said, tucking a bit of hair behind her ear. If they were in a movie, this would be the part where they kissed for the first time. Thank goodness Tara wasn't so star struck to think something like that would really happen.

Beau grinned and nodded toward his truck where Dixie quietly waited by the passenger side. "I think Dixie did too. Thanks for coming out."

"Oh, any time. It was great to catch up with you too."

A few beats of silence passed as they gazed at one another, completely oblivious to the world around them. The nightly chorus of crickets in the woods just on the edge of the parking lot nearly drowned out the sounds of carnival fun.

"I was wondering," Beau began and Tara had to restrain herself from taking a step forward. "Would you like to come over to the ranch tomorrow? Maybe in the afternoon and then we can all have dinner? I don't know if you or Daniel hang out at all, but I'm sure he wouldn't mind reminiscing about high school for a while with you."

All? Tara tried not to feel crest fallen. Somehow, she had hoped Beau was about to ask her out on a real date, just the two of them. Now, he was bringing in Dixie and her dad. Although the idea of poking around the ranch and taking a walk down memory lane was tempting, the idea of spending more time with Beau is what pushed her to nod.

"Sure. I'd love to. It's the Bremor Ranch, right?"

Beau nodded. "Yeah. Here, let me get your number and I'll text you the address."

Tara gladly pulled out her phone and he did the same. They exchanged numbers and he quickly punched out the address for her. Now, she had his number. She had some other line of communication and, though she could already find him on social media, she wasn't about to go on and friend him out of the blue. Her momma taught her better manners and somehow, she would squeeze it into the conversation tomorrow.

"So, I'll see you tomorrow then," Beau said with a smile before he turned to walk away. Tara stood, watching him leave just as he angled back around. "By the way, wear something warm and maybe an extra change of clothes."

"Why?" she laughed.

"You'll see."

With that, he disappeared to the driver side of his truck and Tara realized she was still standing in the middle of the lane, looking like a dumbstruck idiot. She pinched her lips together to keep herself from grinning too hard. Her cheeks were already aching from all the laughing she had done earlier that evening.

She hurried away to her car and as soon as the doors were locked and heater on, she pulled the book out of her purse to skim through the pages.

Sure enough, an entire chapter had manifested, detailing the wonderful night at the carnival in perfect clarity. Yet, it was told from the heroine's perspective. Not once had the story been told from the guy's point of view, which was not the usual way romances were written. There was usually a good mix of both views so the reader could understand what both characters were thinking. She was no writer, but as an avid reader, she knew that much.

Yet, this mysterious and magical book only told Tara what she already knew. That she was falling hard for the compassionate cowboy.

CHAPTER THREE

As soon as Beau opened the door, Dixie squeezed through to scamper down the hall, arms brimming with the prizes they had won at the carnival.

"Daddy! Daddy! Look what we won!" she cried as she ducked into Daniel's office. Beau dropped his keys into the little bowl on the sideboard by the front door and heard Daniel indulge Dixie as she rambled on and on about their time at the festival.

If Beau weren't an adult, he might have been just as effusive with his recounting of the evening, but his focus would have been on their lovely lady companion than on the many rides and games. He could have gone on and on about her hazel eyes, her seductive curves and the way her voice wrapped around his head like a heady perfume. Of course, he couldn't say any of that to Daniel.

He heard his name spoken a few times, but Tara's name came up far more frequently and he wasn't at all surprised to see Daniel come into the kitchen. Dixie was already in the middle of showing her stuffed toys their new home and introducing them to the others piled up in her room. While Beau was searching through the fridge for a snack, his older brother leaned against the doorway.

"So who's Tara?" he asked in an insinuating voice.

Beau grabbed the leftover burrito he stashed in one of the drawers. He had to hide it in a lettuce bag to keep Dixie from snatching it during one of her own snack searches. Apparently she inherited her veracious appetite from her uncle.

"You know her," he said, trying to mask the mild disappointment in his voice. "She works at the dentist office on Main Street."

He straightened and looked at the befuddled look on his brother's face. Daniel was still the mountain of a man he used to be in high school, and still as good looking. He was the superstar he had always been and Beau was forever in his brother's shadow.

"You mean that blonde chick? Rebecca?"

Beau turned away, a little indignant that he wouldn't remember a knockout like Tara. "No, the other one."

There was a long pause before he replied, "Oh... She's cute, I guess."

Cute? Guess? If Beau thought he could get away with throwing a punch or two at his brother, he would have.

"So why was she with y'all tonight?" he continued. "I thought it was just going to be you and Dixie."

Beau put the burrito, still wrapped up, on a paper plate and popped it in the microwave. "I met her at the coffee shop and I just thought she'd be able to help Dixie have a good time, that's all."

He turned and folded his arms before giving his brother a challenging look, daring him to probe deeper into his personal life. He hadn't cared much before now, but maybe that was because it never involved Dixie.

"Well, I'd say she did a good job of that," he replied with a laugh. "I haven't seen her this excited in a while."

Beau saw the dark circles under Daniel's eyes. "Got a headache?" he asked, knowing that look by heart.

Daniel shrugged, probably unwilling to

admit his weakness like always. "I took something earlier. It's fine."

They talked business while the burrito heated up. Though it really wasn't anything Beau needed to know, Daniel told him about the plans for moving the cattle to another pasture in the following week, and all the other little things with the horses and the ranch hands that they employed.

He wasn't sure why Daniel thought to include him on everything. He had never been interested in ranch business, even when their parents were alive. But he would let Daniel talk until he was blue in the face because he certainly didn't need to tell Dixie about any of this stuff. She cared even less than Beau did.

Beau slipped the burrito from the microwave, but allowed it to cool before peeling back the wrapper. "By the way," he said after taking the first bite that slightly burned his tongue, "I invited Tara for dinner tomorrow."

It took a moment for Daniel to switch gears, so he could fully comprehend the words and then his brows shot up. "You invited her for dinner?"

Beau opened his mouth and moved the chunk of burrito around in an attempt keep it from scalding his tongue further. Since he was unable to speak, he only nodded.

"That's pretty serious for a second date, isn't it?"

It was a good thing his mouth was full, so he could formulate a good response to that question. Already, Daniel was assuming that Beau wanted Tara for himself. Dixie probably assumed the same, judging by her question while they waited at the carnival. He had to put a stop to that incorrect thinking before it went too far and Tara became off limits to everyone who really needed her.

Once he swallowed, he said, "She wanted to check out the ranch. We talked about it a little and when I said you were running the show, she seemed pretty eager to come visit. Dixie liked the idea too."

It wasn't completely a lie, but perhaps eighty-percent of it was. Tara showed far more interest in Beau's job on the oil rig than she did in the family business. And Dixie enjoyed her company enough that a second evening with her wouldn't be turned down if Beau told her about it.

It was all to make Daniel at ease about the idea of a stranger coming into his home. If he thought Tara could be a good fit for the ranch and his family, then maybe he wouldn't be so turned off to the idea of her becoming a more permanent part of their lives. It was worth a shot anyway.

Daniel seemed intrigued by the idea and nodded. "Okay... Well, I guess we can saddle up a few of the horses and take her down to see the cattle for a while. I assume you have a meal picked out?"

Beau waved him off. "Don't worry about a thing, except making Tara feel at home."

His brother scoffed. "She's your date, Beau. That's your job."

Again, he had to set things to right. "She's as much my date as she is yours and the ranch's."

Dixie came prancing through the doorway to stand between the men, still wearing all of her evening coats and scarf that she neglected to take off when they came home.

"Tara's coming?" she asked eagerly.

Daniel walked over and began to shell the layers of jackets and sweaters that Beau realized might have been a bit excessive.

"Yep, she's coming over tomorrow," Daniel returned. "So be on your best behavior."

The eight-year-old proceeded to chatter about all the things she wanted to show Tara when she arrived and all the things they could do together in the evening. Beau smiled, glad that at least the little girl could be won over so easily. Daniel was a harder nut to crack, but Beau knew as soon as Tara gave him one of her award-winning, breathtaking smiles, he'd be long gone.

Tara's car rocked side to side, bobbing with the divots and bumps on the dirt road that led to the massive expanse of ranchland. Rolling hills of green grass stretched out beyond her windshield and she could just barely see the dark and light speckles of cattle roaming in the fields. Acres upon acres were bordered by dense lines of shrubbery and picket fencing.

The view from her car alone was breathtaking, but it wasn't the scenery that made her chest ache and stomach flutter with butterflies. She was eager for another reason entirely. Reading back over everything that had happened at the carnival the night before was astounding to say the least. It was as if she were reliving every moment all over again. And she couldn't wait to get home that night to read about everything that would happen on the Bremor ranch today.

On the crest of one of the hills, she could

see the house and barn come into view. A two story marvel with a wrap-around porch. It's the kind of house Tara always imagined would be the home of a wealthy rancher. A few trucks were pulled up near the front, their tires speckled with mud. They must have belonged to the ranch hands that she could just barely hear shouting at the cattle, their voices drifting on the wind.

The barn, just to the south side of the house, was like something out of a painting. She could definitely get used to living on a piece of land like this. The cherry on top came riding up the path, a black cowboy hat hiding his dark wavy hair and strong hands clutching the reins.

Tara's mouth watered at the sight of him and his muscles that were hugged so tightly by his dark shirt. It was clear he had been working hard all day by the way the sweat glistened off his arms and face. The material of his neckline was darkened by that same sweat and she remembered how amazing he smelled in the coffee shop. She couldn't wait to take another whiff.

Beau smiled and she slowed the car to a stop just as he and his chestnut brown horse – the same horse on the book cover - came trotting closer. He briefly let go of the reins so he could touch the brim of his hat in greeting. Her window was already down so she simply poked her head out.

"Where should I park?" she asked over the light roar of the engine.

The horse threw its head a bit as Beau pulled him to a halt. "Over there is fine," he said as he pointed towards the herd of trucks. "You did bring a change of clothes, right?"

Tara confidently nodded. "Yep. Though, I still don't understand what I'd need them for."

Beau chuckled, a deep throaty sound that almost blended in with the purr of the engine. "You'll see."

And she did. When Beau steered away and kicked his steed into a trot to get out of the way, her eyes fell on an area just near the barn. Tied up, saddled, and grazing on the patches of grass between the fence posts, were three beautiful horses. If Beau was already riding his that meant those horses were waiting for her, Dixie, and Daniel.

The twisting in her gut intensified at the thought that Beau wanted them all to go riding together.

Tara parked the car and glanced down at her silky sleeveless blouse and tight jeans that hugged her curves. If she had known he was going to take her riding, she would have stopped at the store and bought a pair of boots or something.

Tara hadn't gone horseback riding since she was a kid on her uncle's farm in Fort Hood. Even then, she was pretty sure it was a miniature pony and they never left the corral. This was the real deal and even Dixie was given a fully matured horse.

She stepped out of the car and the pungent odor of horse manure, hay, and the great outdoors hit her in the face a little harder than she expected. Luckily, her disgusted face was wiped away as soon as Beau reemerged, this time, without the horse. He must have dismounted near the barn.

"Horseback riding?" Tara questioned flirtatiously.

Looking slightly sheepish, he nodded. "Yeah, Dixie loves going out to see the cattle every now and again and I promised I'd take her today. It won't take too long, and then we'll come back to the house for dinner."

Tara appreciated that the plans were not left up to her. All she could do was smile and shrug. "Sounds great to me."

"Tara!"

Dixie came peeling around the side of the house, cowgirl boots pounding into the dirt as she went. A little flock of chickens came running after her and diverted in circles as if they had been spooked by the girl.

She ran up and hugged Tara around the waist. One thing could be said about the little girl. She was resilient. At her age, Tara couldn't imagine going through the traumatic event of losing her mother. She knew for a fact, though, that she wouldn't have been handling it this well.

"Ready to go riding?" Tara asked.

Dixie took her hand and dragged her towards the massive animals. They looked so much bigger up close. "Let me introduce you!" she cried.

With Beau as the silent spectator – again – Dixie presented Tara with the horses they would be taking out into the pastures.

"This one," she said, pointing to a black and white speckled mare, "is Magpie. She's really sweet and loves sugar cube treats." She moved to the brown and tan stallion that seemed a little taller than the other two by a couple of hands. "This is Rex. He's my daddy's horse."

The white mare nuzzled its muzzle at Dixie's shoulder and snorted. "This is Star.

She's my horse. Daddy gave her to me on my sixth birthday."

"Fifth," Beau corrected. "Remember, that was the same year you got the dollhouse."

Dixie's smile faltered a bit and then she nodded. "Oh, right. I knew that. Mom painted that dollhouse for me. Wanna see it?"

Tara bit her lip, completely unsure how to respond to her effusiveness. She wanted to smack Beau for bringing up Dixie's mom when the little girl was so excited. But she refrained and kept her hands tucked away in her back pockets, hoping Beau's attention would be drawn there.

It wasn't that she didn't want to see the dollhouse – she did. It had more to do with the fact that she was still trying to get a handle on the idea that they would be going out horseback riding. "Maybe after we're done riding. Not right now."

Dixie ushered the two adults into the barn and proceeded to introduce Tara to all the other horses that were being stabled there by some of the occupants of Brooksdale, those who didn't have the space to properly house a horse. She raddled on and on about their feeding schedules, what they do to clean them, and all the little things in between that Tara wouldn't have normally cared about. Because it mattered to Dixie, she paid attention and tried to remember everything.

A pair of boots shuffled through the hay at the open double doors that led out of the barn and Tara turned to see Daniel Bremor approach. He was strong and well built, but Tara couldn't get past the slightly sour look that seemed to be permanently fixed on his face. From what she remembered of him in high school, he never looked this unpleasant. She wondered if it had anything to do with losing his wife or the stress of running a ranch. It could even have been losing his parents, which made him have to move back after college.

He was polite enough from the few times he had come to the dentist and Tara thought he was all right, but certainly not the same man he had been in high school. Beau wasn't either and it made her wonder what others could see in her.

Daniel tipped his cowboy hat in the same way that Beau had. He looked cleaner than his brother, his clothes free of stains or any sign that he had stepped out of the house all day. He probably hadn't.

"I see Dixie's talking your ear off," he said and his lips gently curled into a soft smile.

Tara shook her head. "Not at all. It's amazing to see a kid so excited about something."

Daniel nodded and stuck his hands in his pockets before regarding his brother. "At least someone around here is," he said rather pointedly. "We ready to go?"

She looked from Beau to Daniel and back again and saw a silent exchange of looks that told her there must have been some sort of brotherly teasing taking place that she wasn't privy to. Maybe if she could get one of them alone, she could ask.

"Dixie's not done with her tour yet," Beau replied. "She still has to name all the chickens."

At the mention of chickens, Dixie bolted out of the barn. "Yeah!" she squealed. "Come see the chickens!"

Tara giggled and followed at a jogging pace, glad she at least wore her sneakers. The complete tour of the barn and chicken coup continued and soon, Tara met the other residents of the ranch. A basset hound and black lab came bounding in from wherever it was they had been hiding.

Barking up a storm of excitement, they greeted Tara with slobbery nuzzles and the lab tried to prop his paws on her chest. It was a good thing she brought the extra change of clothes, even if she wasn't going riding later. The mud and dirt from the dogs transferred onto her light blue blouse and the moment Beau saw, he made a face of regret. He then proceeded to try and order the pup down, but the lab didn't hear a word since Tara encouraged the show of canine affection.

"We'll put that through the wash when you change later," he said apologetically.

Tara laughed and scratched behind the dog's ears. "No worries. It's dry clean only, anyway."

Dixie squatted to wrap her arms around the fleshy neck of the basset hound. "This is Sherlock and that's Watson."

She nodded her approval of the names, though she wouldn't have named the black lab after the short pudgy sidekick to the beloved literature genius.

Daniel came up and as soon as Watson caught sight of him, he jumped down from Tara. "I'm sorry about him. He gets a little over excited with strangers."

Once more, Tara brushed it off – and the paw prints on her blouse - and turned to Dixie. "Who else haven't I met?"

Dixie thought for a moment and then looked to her dad and uncle. "Can we show her the cows now?"

Beau clapped his hands and rubbed them together. "Ready to go when you are!"

Dixie gave another shout and ran off to where the horses were tied up, the two dogs hurrying after her and barking again. Sherlock had a hard time keeping up, though, and it was rather comical to watch. Tara fell in between the two men as they followed.

"Rocky's tied up at the gate," Beau said. "I'll meet you over there."

With that, he jogged away and left Daniel and Tara to walk alone. She didn't know what to do with the silence that stretched between them. Her first impulse was to give her condolences about his wife, but she knew that was definitely out of the question. They didn't socialize in the same circles in high school and the few times he had come into the dentist office weren't enough to really know a person, much less earn the right to get overly personal.

Luckily, she wouldn't have to start the conversation.

"Dixie told me you and Beau had a great time at the carnival last night."

She nodded. "Oh, yeah. We had a blast."

Daniel's lips broke into another one of those half smiles. "Yeah, she wouldn't stop talking about it while we were trying to put her to bed. You really made an impression on her."

Tara didn't know if she should have been flattered. She looked to the ground ahead of her. "I'm glad she had fun. That's the important part. Kids need a bit of fun every once and a while."

It sounded so lame and off-handed, like she didn't really know the first thing about kids but made a half-hearted attempt at it. She tried not to wince at her own blunder.

Daniel gave a short laugh. "Oh, she has a lot of fun around here. If she's not tormenting the chickens, then she's trying to dress up Sherlock in tutus, or sneaking away to ride her horse. Thankfully, Beau keeps the saddles out of reach now."

Tara giggled and was surprised to see Dixie already astride Star and steering her away from the fence. She wondered how a little girl like her could even reach the stirrups, before she spotted the five-gallon bucket tipped upside down next to the fence railing. She certainly was resourceful. Beau might have to find another way to hide the saddles from her.

"Come on!" she urged.

"Be patient, Dixie," Daniel chided as he walked with Tara to Magpie. The two-tone horse gave her a lazy look, as if she didn't care if the human rode her at all. "Let me help you with that."

Tara gave a brief, wary look at Daniel before she struggled to get her left foot in the stirrup. Her pants were so tight that they barely allowed for any movement in her knees and calves. Looser jeans would have been a better choice.

Daniel took some liberties and elevated her foot for her, gently gripping her ankle to move her into place. With another boost on her other foot, Tara somehow managed to situate herself in the saddle. Magpie shifted her weight from one hoof to the other and Tara tried to balance herself.

"Have you ridden before?" Daniel asked as he adjusted the stirrups to account for her long legs.

Tara swallowed hard and tried to decide how much she should tell him. "Well, it's been a long time."

Daniel fastened the last buckle on her right stirrup and patted Magpie's rump. "She's gentle. You shouldn't have any problems with her."

Tara leaned over a bit to cast Magpie a worried look. "I definitely don't have a problem with her, but what if she has a problem with me?"

He laughed, this time a little more heartily as he moved to the darker horse, Rex. "She actually belongs to a family up the road that's on vacation right now. We're boarding her and two other horses while they're away. They offer beginner riding lessons, so it's safe to say Magpie will take care of you."

Tara was thankful for their thoughtfulness in picking her horse. Not knowing her experience with riding, surely it was Beau's idea to give her an easy horse.

Some stuff came back to her pretty quickly. She understood that pulling back on the reins made Magpie stop, kicking her made her go faster, and the simple directions. Getting the fine tuning of everything else was a little harder and Tara found she was less than graceful trying to find the perfect balance as the saddle lilted side to side with each step.

Now was her chance to ask about what Daniel had said earlier. "When you were talking about how much Dixie loves the ranch, did I notice a little teasing between you and Beau?"

Daniel steered his horse closer and they stopped just before rounding the corner of the house where the others were waiting. By the way he took a breath and leaned against his saddle horn, Tara could tell that whatever he had to say might have been a little too personal.

"You don't have to answer that," she countered quickly. "I don't want to pry."

Daniel shook his head, a kind of modesty in his countenance that she wasn't used to seeing in him. "No, it's fine. When we were growing up, Beau never really liked the ranch. Neither did I, but I didn't argue with my parents about it nearly as much. It was something he and our dad fought about a lot. That's why he moved away from Brooksdale and why he wasn't included in the will when our parents died. The ranch was given solely to me and our dad made sure that Beau would never profit from it whatsoever."

Tara's shoulders slumped. All this time, she suspected that they co-owned the ranch somehow. It would have made sense, but she never imagined that Beau was on bad terms with his parents. She thought perhaps he had moved away because of the job opportunity or some weird blue-collar career dream he had growing up. To think there was strife in the Bremor home shed a new light on her high school years. While Beau was the meek kid in the back of the class and Daniel was star of the football team, their home life was fraught with conflict over a family business that didn't want to be continued.

Knowing that, coupled with the fact that

Beau actually did come back to help his brother and niece, added a whole new facet to his psychology that made Tara want him even more.

"If you don't like it, why don't you just sell it? I bet there are tons of people looking for land like this."

Daniel shook his head vehemently like it was absolutely impossible to even conceive of such a plan. "Nope. This ranch has been passed down for generations. I'm already thinking that Dixie can have it when she grows up, if she still wants it. That was our parents' wish, to keep it in the family. And I want to respect their wishes."

Just like Beau, Daniel seemed to be just as loyal and selfless. She smiled in admiration. "I suppose there's nothing wrong with that, then."

All four riders met at the gate. Dixie and Beau led the way while Daniel and Tara followed, though she would have much preferred to be beside Beau. The path didn't exactly allow for three horses to walk abreast of one another.

Dixie filled the void of conversation pretty quickly and none of the adults tried to stop her, though, Daniel occasionally tried to cut in and make small talk with Tara as they made their way out to the pasture.

He tried to ask how her job at the dentist office was going and the good ole days of their high school years. She played nice and asked him questions in return, though her eyes were fixed on Beau and how he rhythmically swayed in his saddle. She never thought it would be possible for a man to look so sexy riding a horse, but Beau definitely proved her wrong. She might not have been right beside him the whole way, but the view of his back muscles had that tender space between her legs tingling. And the way the saddle was rubbing there... well, it was a good thing she brought an extra pair of panties as well.

Despite the slight awkwardness of getting on her horse and feeling out of place as a guest at the ranch, Tara was enjoying herself. Once they were a good distance away from the barn, she felt she could savor the fresh air and the glorious cultured wilderness around them. For a girl who lived in Texas her whole life, she rarely made it out into the countryside. One thing or another detained her and she learned to settle for the perfectly worded scenery descriptions in her favorite books, as opposed to experiencing it in person.

It didn't take them long to find the cattle. All four of them lined up atop the crest of the hill that overlooked the pasture she had passed on her way up the road.

Dixie and Beau were quiet while Daniel explained everything they did on the ranch to ensure the cattle were properly cared for. Though Dixie called them cows, the horns and obvious bulk to their frame showed that they were not the milking kind.

Half of what Daniel said went in one ear and out the other, though she tried to keep up with all the arduous chores the ranch hands were tasked with each day. It certainly wasn't a breeze running a big operation like this.

"And what do you do to keep all this running smoothly?" Tara asked the younger brother.

Beau shifted in his saddle, the leather creaking with the movement. "I help the ranch hands where it's needed." His tone betrayed his general indifference to the whole thing, but Tara still admired his resolve to lend a hand.

Daniel moved to her left. "I used to do that, too. But, I've been having to take care of a lot of paperwork instead. Someone has to balance the books."

Tara's curiosity prompted her to ask why the switch in positions, but she knew very well what must have instigated it and she wasn't about to ask that in Dixie's company. This family dynamic was getting more complicated by the minute and she was suddenly thankful for her quiet, slightly dull life.

"Can we get closer?" the little girl asked eagerly.

Beau blew out his cheeks and nodded. "I suppose we can. Want a closer look at the cattle? I can show you that brand Daniel was talking about."

The idea of getting closer to the cattle stench was not on her top list of things to do that evening. Tara nodded, knowing that Dixie wanted to go down there. And just maybe if she showed the right amount of interest, Beau would like her all the better for it.

The three experienced riders prodded their horses to make their way down the hill and Tara did the same. However, what she wasn't accounting for was the deep slope she would have to compensate for. Magpie did excellent at keeping up with the rest, but Tara found herself struggling to lean back while keeping an adequate hold on the reins with her feet fixed in the stirrups.

She wasn't sure if Magpie stumbled a bit, or if the horse's extreme, rocking steps were what did it, but Tara was finally thrown off kilter. Unable to right herself, she fell to the side. Foolishly, she kept a tight hold on Magpie's reins. The horse was just as surprised as the human was.

They both gave out a cry and one of her feet became dislodged in the fall. Her other ankle twisted in the occupied stirrup, but not in a painful way. What was more painful was the way she face-planted into the dirt.

The reins slipped from her hands and the horse obediently came to a stop just when Tara realized why her chest hadn't hit solid ground. The smell was the first giveaway.

Her face puckered in revulsion as a light swarm of flies buzzed out of the way. She heard the two men dismount and come to her aid. Daniel set to work getting her foot free from the stirrup while Beau helped her to stand.

The entire front of her blouse, once a pretty blue like the clear Texas sky, was now coated in a thick layer of dung. The cow patty had broken her fall, but she would have much rather felt the hard impact of the ground knocking the wind out of her than this.

Despite that, Tara caught herself smiling. It was utterly embarrassing, humiliating, and disgusting, but it was too funny not to laugh at herself.

"Are you all right?" Beau asked, and she could see the smile play on his lips like he was ready to burst out in a laugh too.

"I'm fine," she giggled, "but I think I'm ready to go change clothes now."

Dixie rode back over and watched. Taking Tara's lead, she laughed as well. Daniel didn't find it nearly as amusing and shushed his daughter.

"I'm so sorry," he said, taking Magpie by the reins to keep her from running off. "I thought she would have been a good horse for you."

Tara waved him off and looked to a bit of the thick brown sludge that had smeared across the skin on her arms and chest. "She was. I just lost my balance."

"Not used to riding?" Beau questioned.

Tara gave him a pitiful shake of her head, but the smile wouldn't go away. "Would you mind if I took a shower, too?"

Beau grinned. "Sure. We should have some women's body wash left in the guest bathroom."

Such a comedic moment couldn't be spoiled by that somber thought that they did have lady bathroom amenities, but no lady left in the house. Tara considered it luck that they hadn't thrown it away yet.

When she went back to read this scene in the book, Tara knew she'd get a good laugh out of it again. Maybe once the stench left her nose, it would be even funnier. Though, she would never forget the way the cow patty was still pretty warm when she landed in it. And she'd gladly do it again if it meant that Beau would touch her arm again the way he did when he helped her back up the hill.

CHAPTER FOUR

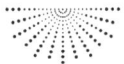

Beau was no stranger to stains like these. He remembered once how Dixie had fallen into a cow patty just as massive. Though, when his niece got dirty, they would just hose her down in the yard before bringing her inside. Beau couldn't reasonably do that with Tara, though part of him wished he could have seen her all wet like that.

Instead, he settled for snatching her dirty clothes from her outstretched hand that she slipped through the cracked bathroom door. The knowledge that she was standing naked in his shower was enough to make him rock hard while he went to the mudroom, gently scrubbed off the dung and muck from her blouse.

Seeing Tara get along so well with Dixie

had been a treat. He had dated plenty of women who pretty much treated his niece like a baby whenever he brought them to meet the rest of his family. Tara didn't do that. She almost treated Dixie like an equal.

When Daniel came out with his usual sour face, Beau thought about giving him a piece of his mind. How was he supposed to impress Tara when he barely smiled and only talked about business?

After getting the last of the mud off her blouse, Beau threw it, along with her jeans and underwear – a black lacy thing that must have gotten a little sweaty during the ride – in the washing machine set on a delicate cycle. He wasn't an expert on washing a lady's clothes. Most of the time, he had to put the cycle on heavy-duty just to get the dust and dirt out of his jeans.

Daniel appeared in the doorway to the laundry room, his hands jammed in his jean pockets. Everyone else had changed and Dixie was busy looking through her closet of board games to find something for the family to do before dinner.

Beau looked up into his brother's eyes and knew something was troubling him – more than usual.

"What's up?" he asked, folding his arms over his chest.

Daniel let out a long breath. "She didn't seem all that interested in the ranch. And I can't believe you made her ride without making sure she was comfortable with it. Is there another reason you invited her here? I mean, I don't mind if you like her, but you don't have to make up stuff."

Beau lowered his brows. "I didn't make up a story. She really seemed to want to come over."

His brother donned that look that told Beau he wasn't buying it anymore. Why did Daniel have to be so suspicious? Could he just fall in love with Tara the moment they locked eyes? Why couldn't this be easy?

Truth be told, Beau saw the hesitance in Tara's eyes when she realized all of them would go riding together, as if she were disappointed somehow. Beau had brushed it off after he saw how awkward she behaved on Magpie while they were riding out to the pastures. How was he supposed to know that she wouldn't know how to ride or handle a horse? She was perfect in every other way. But when she seemed to brighten up after he escorted her back to the house, just the two of them, Beau thought he had a better idea why.

It seemed that both Tara and Daniel were going to make this match-making game difficult for him.

With a little sheepish shrug, he said, "I wanted you to meet her. She's a great girl and..." He paused, trying to think of a way out of this mess. Maybe there was another angle he could approach this from, one that wouldn't make Daniel throw up his guard. "I thought she might be a good bookkeeper for the ranch or a nanny for Dixie. I know you need help around here, so I was just trying to look out for some potential candidates."

Daniel seemed to buy his white lie again, only partially satisfied with his excuse. His brother might have not been the smart one, but he had some common sense when it came to business. He knew what was sound logic and what was a bad idea. He always said it had something to do with what his gut told him. Luckily, that same gut wasn't a lie detector.

"I guess she might be good for a bookkeeper. She's got experience at the dentist office. And Dixie likes her, so maybe she could do both... I thought this had to do with you and her."

If Daniel was going to ever entertain the idea of Tara being a future wife, Beau had to lie again. At least he wasn't mad about Beau supposedly overstepping his bounds. And he was thankful his brother didn't ask why he suddenly cared about the wellbeing of the ranch at all. "What?" he replied with as much disgust as he could muster when thinking about Tara. "No. She's not my type."

His brother cocked an eyebrow at him. "Not your type? How can she not be your type?"

Yeah, he was going to have to lie big time. "I don't know... I guess it's her legs."

Daniel's eyes nearly popped out. "Her legs?"

"Too long."

At that, he snorted and turned away. "You've lost your mind."

This was a good sign and Beau resisted the urge to smile. Though her legs were a huge plus to her overall stunning looks, Beau tried to pick out something he knew Daniel would disagree with. Daniel always loved long legs.

Before he could continue, Dixie came running up with a deck of playing cards. "Daddy, can we play Texas Hold 'Em before dinner?"

Daniel ruffled the top of his daughter's head. "Who taught you to play that?"

Beau saw this as his cue and slipped out

behind his brother to retreat down the hall just as his niece was throwing him under the bus.

TARA WRINGED her hair dry and stepped out of the shower, water dripping from her skin, soaking the towel that had been laid out in lieu of a bath mat. The water pressure in Beau's bathroom was much better than in her own apartment and it made her look forward to the possibility of showering there more often.

While she washed away the dirt and grime from the ride, scrubbing her skin until she couldn't smell the cow dung anymore, Tara thought of nothing else but the lovely evening ahead. When they came inside, she heard Dixie say something about playing a game before dinner. She wasn't one for games, mostly because she could get insanely competitive by accident. However she'd do just about anything to spend more time with Beau.

She found a clean towel underneath the counter and breathed in the scent of clean linen to detox her nostrils after the harrowing ordeal she'd had on the horse. With time, she was sure she could get used to living on a ranch. Hell, she might even enjoy going for long evening rides with Beau every so often.

She'd probably have to if she ever hoped to be in a real relationship with him.

It was then that the harsh reality hit her in the face. She and Beau weren't dating. Not really. She wasn't exactly sure where she stood with him. Dixie loved her, that was a fact, but a child's admiration seemed a lot easier to win right now than Beau's. There was the softness of his touch and the hungry way he looked at her sometimes, but besides that, there was nothing else to prove his affections. She wasn't really even sure how to find out without blatantly asking him, which was out of the question anyway.

She dried her body and hair to the best of her ability and then slipped on a fresh set of clothes. Not wishing to be wasteful, she wrapped her used towel around her shoulders to keep her damp hair off her clothes. She exited the bathroom, letting steam roll out with her. Not only was the water pressure phenomenal, but she could turn it to the perfect temperature.

When she stepped out into Beau's bedroom, she took a moment to look around, searching for anything that could tell her more about him. With the stench of cow shit still clinging to her skin, she didn't want to waste a lot of time wandering around.

A pair of jeans were thrown over the foot-board and she saw the back pockets were speckled with dirt and hay. Maybe he intended to wear them later? Next to his digital alarm clock, she could see the prong-end of a phone charger and a rather fancy looking wrist watch that laid undone across the surface. It was definitely too clean and formal to wear when he was out working with the livestock. Maybe he only wore it for special occasions? The idea of Beau in anything but Wranglers was a little hard to imagine, but she wouldn't mind seeing him in a nice suit and jacket.

The walls were bare, but that wasn't too surprising. If he had just moved in a few months ago, he probably didn't have the time or the motivation to get too settled and person-alize the room. His closet wasn't crowded at all. His wardrobe was sparse in comparison to hers. Only maybe half a dozen button-down shirts, and some polos. No sign of that formal suit.

Tara ran her fingers over the smooth leather fabric of a jacket sleeve and noticed there were several shoe and packing boxes covering the floor of the closet. If only she had the time and privacy to leaf through and see what secrets they held.

This couldn't have been everything he brought with him from his previous place.

Could this room have belonged to him before he left home the first time? This hardly looked to be the room of a teenage boy that would have been kept in pristine condition by loving parents. Then again, with the rocky history between Beau and his family, maybe they wanted to wipe out all remembrance of him. That would explain the minimalist décor and lack of possession.

The chest of drawers must have held his t-shirts, jeans, and other clothes that most people didn't bother to hang up in a closet. She wondered if the book would retell this moment and give her hints to whatever hidden contents were in the drawers.

Remembering the book reminded her that there was so much left unspoken in this story. She still didn't know Beau's side and so desperately wanted to know what he thought of her. He seemed interested, but she wasn't about to go probing for answers to him personally. There had to be some way to get him alone, without Daniel or Dixie so she could better assess what it was they shared.

She bit her lip as a clever plan formed in her mind. Then again, could she even do anything? So far, she had let Beau and the book dictate what was happening day to day. How much freedom was she granted when it came to throwing in a plot twist or moving this romance forward the way she wanted it to go?

She jumped just as the bedroom door opened and Beau appeared. Spinning in place, caught in the act of staring into his closet again, she was suddenly too shy to say a thing. Did he suspect that she was looking at his stuff? Would he be mad?

He seemed to recover from the shock of seeing her there, barefoot with a towel draped over her shoulders, and smiled. "Have a nice shower?"

Oh, what she wouldn't have given to know if he would ever say those exact words to her again, but under different – more pleasurable – circumstances. While she rinsed her hair, she couldn't help but realize that the shower stall was just big enough for two people to squeeze in. That made her mind run wild with ideas.

She nodded and hoped that her cheeks didn't turn too red under the question. "Yeah, thanks for letting me use your bathroom."

"Anytime."

Tara forced herself not to read into that response. He was just being nice. No need to get excited. Though, she could already tell that a bit of heat was pooling between her legs.

Beau cleared his throat and she wondered if he realized his slip. "Have you ever played

Texas Hold 'Em before?" he asked as he jerked a thumb toward the door.

She blinked at the question, unsure of how to respond. "Ummm... I think I played it once or twice during summer camp, but not recently."

Beau's smile reached his eyes. "Well, I think Dixie may want to teach you. She's been shuffling the cards for the last ten minutes."

Somehow, Tara had expected whatever game they played would involve dice, moving pieces around a board, and laughing across a table. Cards hadn't even entered her mind. "I hope I wasn't leaving y'all waiting for too long."

"No, Dixie's just impatient. When we're done with a few rounds, we'll start dinner."

Tara walked closer after retrieving her bag from the bathroom. "What's on the menu, by the way?"

"Spaghetti. Dixie's way."

She made a face. "Should I be scared?"

Beau chuckled as he leaned a bit on the doorknob. "No, not at all. It's actually pretty good."

"When you said it was Dixie's kind of spaghetti, I half expected the sauce would be ketchup or something."

He laughed as she came to the door and they stood so close to one another that she could smell that clean linen scent on his shirt that matched his towels. "Believe it or not, she is picky about her spaghetti. You won't have to worry about anything unusual in your sauce."

Tara smiled and let this moment seep in as she looked up into Beau's gorgeous blue eyes and saw how the outside corners crinkled when he laughed. It was like he made everything perfect, just by being this close to her. Why hadn't she paid more attention to him in school? Had she been so shallow as to look him over just because he didn't have big muscles or a jersey uniform? Beau had the heart of a real fairytale hero, but she had passed him up. How could she had been so stupid?

And by the way he looked, he must have felt the same. Oh, how she wished that darn book could have told her what he was feeling right then. She had no idea what to say. Honestly, just to stand so close, sharing the same air, was more than enough to make her ridiculously happy. They could have kissed, or just stood there for a hundred years. As long as he was there, gazing down at her with such kind eyes, Tara didn't care which it was. Surely he did care for her, even a little.

"We probably shouldn't keep Dixie waiting for much longer or she'll start dealing the cards for us. And she cheats, just so you know."

Tara briefly looked away before she giggled again. "Good thing I'm wearing long sleeves so I can slip in a card or two."

Beau gave a playful groan as he closed the door behind him. "Oh, no. Not another cheater."

TARA AND DANIEL had walked out of the house several minutes ago, and Beau's hands were busy washing the dishes from dinner. It was the only thing he could do to distract himself from running to the window the way Dixie had.

The evening couldn't have gone better. Dixie was more than excited to teach Tara Texas Hold 'Em and in turn, she learned just as quickly. If they had been playing with real money instead of Monopoly money, the guys would have been cleaned out within the first three games. The girls dominated.

Dinner went just as smoothly and Beau couldn't remember a time when there had been as much conversation and laughter at the table. They talked about everything from the ranch to Tara's job at the dentist to their old high school days. Old gossip about classmates, teachers, and winning football games were the most exciting topics. Dixie was in for a real treat when they broke out a stack of dusty yearbooks to leaf through. There was a kind of nostalgic pain when they looked to fellow classmates who were voted most likely to succeed or something related, only to find that their lives after high school were so totally different than any of them had imagined.

But the fun feeling was rekindled when they came upon the old line dancing club photos. He had never noticed Tara's picture there before. When he pointed to the photo of her swinging her hips and tapping a pair of boots on a dance floor, she shrugged it off as something she did after school for a while. The picture of her holding a trophy told a different story. Beau watched the way she colored when he said that he'd love to watch her dance sometime. Maybe that was the next step in getting her and Daniel closer.

Talking with Tara was easy. Even Daniel opened up and Beau was sure his brother hadn't been that happy since before the funeral. Everything was falling into place, but Beau's chest continued to ache. Yeah, everything was going according to his secret plans, but that might as well have been a disaster for him. Tara won his heart just as quickly and seamlessly as she had won Dixie's and Daniel's in the timespan of two evenings. How could a woman so perfect and beautiful not be taken already? He couldn't even recall her dating in high school.

If they had a moment alone, he would have asked just that. But, it was his brother's turn to have a moment. If he could have talked to his seventeen-year-old self, he would have threatened him to ask Tara out while he had the chance.

"Do you think daddy's going to ask her out?" Dixie cried from the living room.

Those words were like a branding iron straight through his chest. He dried his hands and went to the front window where Dixie had pulled up a chair to sit in while she spied on her dad. Beau squatted beside her and pulled back the curtain a little more to take a peek.

"Well?" she squealed, practically bouncing in her seat.

Instead of giving his true opinion on the matter, he looked to his niece and asked, "Do you want him to ask her out?"

Dixie grinned and now he knew from whom she inherited that devilish look in her eye. Him. "I do. Daddy laughed a lot tonight. I want him to laugh more and if Tara can do that, I want him to ask her out."

Beau swallowed hard and looked back

outside. Tara and Daniel were quietly talking by her car and though it was too dark to make out their faces, he knew they were standing rather close to one another.

He wished he could have been out there, saying goodnight to her. He would take her hands in his, tell her that he had an amazing night, and ask her to share so many more nights with him. He'd kiss those soft, full lips and breathe in the scent of the lavender body wash she had used a few hours ago. If things went well enough, he would have pinned her to the car and made out with her like he wanted to the night before when they stood in the parking lot outside the carnival.

He ran his fingers through his hair and let out a long breath.

"Are you ok, Uncle Beau?" Dixie asked, her voice pulling him back to reality.

Of course he wasn't all right. Tara wasn't his and wouldn't be, if everything went right.

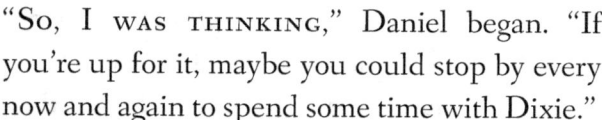

"So, I was thinking," Daniel began. "If you're up for it, maybe you could stop by every now and again to spend some time with Dixie."

Tara smiled, though she really wanted to scream. Dixie was a wonderful girl and a bundle of fun when they were playing cards. She couldn't remember a time when she'd had such a great time, besides maybe the carnival the night before. This night, however, was even more special because she got to sit across from Beau. They occasionally looked up and when their gazes met, it was like fireworks. Every single time. She was falling headlong for Beau, so when it was Daniel who offered to escort her to her car, she wanted to demand that his brother do it instead. That would have been rude, though, so she just politely nodded.

Coming by to play with Dixie every once and a while wasn't such a bad idea, when she thought about it a little more. If she came to the ranch, maybe she'd get a chance to see Beau again. She could stay for dinner more often. She had to twist these things around or else she'd get totally disheartened.

Tara nodded. "I wouldn't mind. I'm sure she'd like the company."

Daniel's hands were tucked deep into his pockets, almost up to his wrists. Strange that they had just been talking about how Daniel scored so many winning touchdowns, but he seemed so nervous around her. "Great. Beau has your number, right?"

"Yep, and I've got his," she replied. "I can also look up your number in our patient directory, so I can get your number that way." Honestly, she didn't want to spend another moment standing by her car. She wanted to hurry home and lose herself in the magical book for a few hours so she could relive the night all over again.

Daniel nodded and something akin to hope sparked in his eyes, but she couldn't figure why. "Okay, that sounds good." He paused, but she could tell by the way he made such solid eye-contact and how his lips parted just a bit, that he had something else he wanted to say. The words just weren't coming out quick enough. "I'm really glad Beau met you, and I hope this hasn't been too awkward at all."

Awkward? How could going on two indirect dates with a guy using the excuse of entertaining his niece ever seem awkward? Tara laughed it off. "Oh, it's fine. Dixie's a great kid and you guys have been so nice, even after I totally embarrassed myself on Magpie earlier."

Daniel smiled, his teeth slightly reflecting the porch light behind her. "I'm sorry about that too. I'm sure after a few more rides, you'll get the hang of it."

That implied there would be more chances to come to the ranch. More chances to see Beau. Maybe, more chances to take a shower after she got sweaty and dirty from a long trail ride. "I'm sure I will."

Daniel took a deep, steeling breath and plunged right into what was weighing on his mind. "So, do you dance anymore? I mean, the line dancing like in the club in high school."

Tara wanted to tear out that page from the yearbook as soon as she saw it. The only reason she even joined that club was because her friends all said she should and it would be a neat way to exercise. It was, and she loved the way those cutoff jeans turned the heads of all the guys in the club, but she didn't do it for long. That was the only competition she had ever entered and then she dropped out of the club the following semester.

But she saw the way Beau slid her an intrigued look, as if he wanted to see her in those cutoff jeans now that she had grown into her long legs a bit. Maybe Daniel was acting on Beau's behalf and covertly asking about line dancing so they could go out. That would have been absolutely perfect.

"Not really, but I'm sure I could remember the steps," she replied with a grin.

He smiled in return, as if that was exactly what he wanted to hear. "Great. I know they do line dancing down at the Howling Moon in Morrisville. Do you want to go with me tomorrow? It's Friday night and I think they'll have a live band."

Tara tried not to let her disappointment show. Daniel was asking her out? If they were in high school, she would have said yes in a heartbeat, just because every girl in her class would have given their right arm to be noticed by the football jock. Now, older and wiser with better tastes, Tara knew she preferred the sport star's younger brother.

But once more, the gears in her mind were turning. She didn't have the book to consult, nor could she spare a moment to think about it. This might have been her big chance to land Beau for good.

"That'd be fun. Can I bring a friend along? She loves dancing too and maybe you can bring Beau along."

Daniel didn't seem totally turned off by the idea. "So, kind of like a double-date?"

Tara would have rather planted face-first in a steaming cow patty than let Rebecca get anywhere close to Beau. Although once she explained the situation, maybe it could be redeemed. She just needed to get Beau alone.

"Yeah, something like that," she replied. "Do you think Beau would go for it?"

"I can definitely ask. I'll talk it over with him tonight and see what he says."

She nodded in agreement. "And I'll ask my friend too. I'm sure she'll say yes, though."

That was a lie. Rebecca was one of her friends who completely refused to step foot on the dance floor no matter if it was at prom, at the homecoming dance, or for the club. She had two left feet and wasn't ashamed to use that as an excuse. Tara was sure that as soon as she mentioned Daniel Bremor was coming along, she'd be onboard for just about anything, including a little honkytonk dancing.

CHAPTER FIVE

THE RHYTHM OF THE HEAVY BASS DRUM rattled the windows of the County Line Bar just outside of Morrisville. The clinging of glasses and rowdy laughter of its patrons leaked through the door as it continually opened and closed to admit more guests or smokers who stepped out for a break. The thirty-minute drive was worth it just for the chance to see Tara again.

When Daniel told Beau that they were all going dancing, he didn't know whether to be ecstatic or crestfallen. Especially when his brother mentioned that Tara would be bringing a date for him. Had he read her wrong from the beginning? It was stupid to be so hopeful that maybe Tara fancied him over Daniel – her intended match – but were all those flirtatious moments just a front? Did she really not like him as he suspected? Or had she changed her mind after meeting Daniel and reminiscing over high school?

But he stopped himself. He couldn't think about all that or it would drive him nuts. Things were going according to plan. The carnival trip and dinner at the ranch were designed to get Tara to test the waters and see if she liked their lifestyle. Now, she was going on a date with Daniel that would hopefully lead to more. Wedding bells could be in their future, but not for Beau. When it came to the moment when Daniel would ask him to be the best man, Beau wasn't sure what he would say. To stand by and watch his older brother get the girl of his dreams might have been too much.

He never anticipated feeling this much for Tara. After they parted ways in high school, he thought they would never see one another again. With nothing in his pockets except a few hundred dollars to get him started and a broken heart to keep him warm at night, Beau thought he wouldn't have to put himself through something like that again. Now, Tara was slowly mending his heart back together without even knowing it, and he had to rip out the stitching as she went.

Beau kicked at a pebble to send it rolling a few yards across the parking lot outside the bar.

"What's got you?" Daniel asked, his thumbs slung in his belt loops as he leaned against the tailgate of his Dodge pickup.

He had his back turned to his brother, so he could make as many pained and angry expressions as he pleased. "Nothing," he said, keeping the agitation out of his words as best he could under the circumstances. "I just don't like the idea of a blind date, you know?"

It was the truth. Tara never mentioned who her friend was, but only that she would be an eager dancer. Beau wasn't too sure he wanted to dance at all tonight, knowing that Tara would be on the floor with Daniel.

"Yeah, I know how you feel," Daniel said. "For your sake, I hope she's cute."

Beau rolled his eyes. Compared to Tara, every girl on the planet was plain and homely.

He spotted Tara's car as it pulled into the parking lot, a little red coupe – the same one she owned in high school. It was already dark and the headlights shined against his legs and torso as they came around to find a parking spot. He shouldn't have been nervous. It wasn't his date. Damn, how he wanted to scream and pound his fists against the hood of a nearby car.

They came walking up a few moments

later and Beau wished he were irresponsible enough to throw away every commitment he had made to his brother's happiness. Tara was wearing a pair of cutoff jeans, despite the dropping mercury. He didn't even look to her friend as she came up, her hips already swinging with each step. Underneath her blue plaid button-down shirt, a white tank top hugged against her trim form, showing off every curve he wished he could explore.

She smiled and the wind tossed her hair back in such a way that made his manhood firm up instantly. Daniel seemed to be just as entranced.

"I hope we weren't making you wait too long," she said.

Beau would have waited a thousand years if it meant he would get to take a deep whiff of whatever expensive perfume she was wearing just then.

"Not long," Daniel replied. His eyes shifted instantly to Tara's blonde friend. "You work at the dentist too, don't you?"

Beau wrenched his thoughts away from Tara and looked to the other girl, whom he recognized now. She and Tara were attached at the hip in their chemistry class and he had seen them hanging out after school quite often.

"Rebecca, right?" he guessed. This must

have been the blonde Daniel had almost mistaken Tara for the other night.

She smiled, but it was a weak one. "That's me."

Somehow, Beau got the idea that Rebecca really didn't want to be there. At least they had that much in common.

When he looked back to the other two, he found that their attentions were a little crossed. Daniel's date was staring at Beau, while Tara's date was ogling Rebecca and the way her off-the-shoulder blouse showed off a little cleavage.

Once more, his mind was split. How could Daniel be gawking at Rebecca while Tara was standing in front of him, looking like a Lonestar Goddess? At the same time, he loved the way her eyes were pouring over him in that same lusty way that made his heart skip a few beats.

Being the better man, he ribbed his brother and offered his elbow to Rebecca. "Come on," he said to her, forcing a smile. "I'll buy you a beer."

That seemed to be enough to snap Daniel back to the evening's agenda and he stepped beside Tara to lead the way toward the door.

"I actually don't drink beer. Do you think they have wine?" Rebecca inquired.

Beau only shrugged and tried not to look down to Tara's fine ass and the way her jeans hugged them so perfectly. "I think so, but you may get some weird looks."

"I can't stand the taste of beer, much less the smell of it. I'd rather have something a little fruity."

Tara looked over her shoulder as Daniel opened the doors to let them in. "Can't you just try a good draft beer or something?"

Rebecca made a face. "I'll stick to what I like, thanks."

Inside the honkytonk, the bar counter was set up on the far left side of the room with half of the rickety stools already taken by couples and friends who were out for a good time. Ahead was the stage where the band had been playing a couple of minutes before. They were taking a break, letting the sound and chatter of everyone else fill the barroom for the moment. Along the other two walls were tables and chairs that were just as unstable and old as the bar itself. Cleared away in the center, rather unceremoniously, was the dancefloor right in front of the stage. Its wooden planks were scuffed by the countless pairs of boots that had stomped, skipped and skidded across their once polished surface.

The neon lights buzzed on the wall as skimpy fans hung motionless above their heads. During the summer, this place could get downright stuffy and hot with all the moving bodies on the dancefloor. The odors of beer and stale cigarette smoke had permeated the floors, walls, and ceiling over the years. He was sure that even if they tore this place down and rebuilt it as something else, it'd smell the same way.

Couples who had been married for decades had met here for their first dates. Men and women in need of companionship and comfort during their darkest hours had come to this place for a little escape from the harsh world. Friends had met there to equally celebrate and mourn. Bartenders came and went. Numerous bands had gotten their start right here and moved on to bigger things. But the owner – a guy that went by the name of King – would never give up County Line Bar, not for all the fortunes in the world, as he put it. It was an iconic spot with its own character, its own sort of life that you could feel as soon as you walked in the door.

Daniel led them toward an empty table and cleared away some of the peanut shell crumbs left behind by a previous group. Beau was already walking toward the bar to place his and Rebecca's order when Daniel was asking for Tara's.

King was at the bar, laughing with a couple of guys about how the bar was founded. It was a story he had heard a thousand times already and he didn't even live in Brooksdale anymore. The old man, his shoulder-length salt and pepper hair pulled back into a thin ponytail, turned to Beau with smiling eyes.

"Hey, man!" he bellowed in greeting. "Haven't seen you around here in a while!"

They shook hands and Beau wondered if he could get away with sitting at the bar all night instead of with the others. It might have been rude, but he couldn't stand to see his brother moving in on the girl he really wanted. Then again, maybe he needed to step in and make sure Daniel didn't get sidetracked with Rebecca.

"I'm just here with my brother on a double-date," he replied. It was pointless to hide it from King. He'd find out anyway.

The bar owner leaned over to get a good look at the girls and whistled. "Damn, son! I don't know which ones yours, but you did good either way."

Daniel arrived just a second or two later before Beau could formulate a response that didn't make him sound bitter or resentful about his arrangement with Rebecca.

"Two beers," his brother said, leaning against the edge of the pitted and polished bar counter. King kept the bar in better condition than his regular tables and it reflected the over-head can lights.

King gave a nod and looked to Beau for his order. When Beau mentioned he wanted a wine and a beer, the owner chuckled.

"I'm gonna assume the wine is for your date," he said with a hearty laugh before turning around to pour their glasses.

Beau elbowed his brother, who was too busy staring back at the two girls at the table. "Eyes off my date," he warned, even though he didn't truly mean it. How he felt a mess of contradicting emotions war in his chest at that moment. It didn't help matters when Tara eyes lifted and she gave him that look that told him his chances of getting somewhere with her were pretty good.

TARA'S MOUTH watered as she checked out Beau's sexy ass in those blue jeans. Damn, how she wished she could have been the one to dance with him. Maybe if they did a line dance, she could at least stand next to him.

Rebecca was not a willing victim of these circumstances. She didn't like bars, didn't like dancing, and didn't even like country music. She had moved to Brooksdale from out east back when she was in middle school, because her parents wanted a change of pace from their hectic, inner city lifestyle. Rebecca probably would have moved out of the small town long ago if it weren't for the amazing friends she had made in school.

Right about now, though, Tara was sure Rebecca wanted to disown her completely.

"At least you get to spend some time with Daniel," she said after Rebecca had mumbled out a string of complaints about the smell of the bar and the loud noise of the band that was tuning up on the stage for another round.

Rebecca shot her a look. "That's the only reason I'm here at all."

Tara watched the boys saunter back with their orders. Poor Beau carried a wine glass for Rebecca, which looked pretty emasculating as it was. She wasn't deterred though. She loved the way his black, tight fitted shirt was tucked behind his big silver belt buckle, which might have been the only thing keeping his pants from falling off his hips.

Daniel handed Tara her beer, but she didn't take a sip right away as the guys did. She might have needed a little something to take the edge off this awkward double-date, but she also didn't want to get carried away and say too much too soon.

Daniel and Rebecca started in on some small talk that Tara followed and occasionally contributed to, but she saw that Beau was fairly quiet in comparison. The way he took swig after swig from his glass, she might have suspected he was trying just as hard to be at ease as she was without the aid of alcohol.

She watched him closely and the way his blue eyes wandered around the room. She had read about this in the book earlier that day at work. Sneaking in a few pages under the table at the desk, Tara had to stop right about this point in the evening. Beyond that, the book wouldn't divulge anything.

She knew she was going to wear the cutoffs, she knew Rebecca was going to complain, she knew the guys would go get their drinks, and she knew that Beau was going to be distracted and slightly listless while they all chatted.

What she didn't know was why. She didn't know what songs the band would play, or what dances would come up next. The rest was up to her and Beau.

The next song came on and she immediately recognized it. Copperhead Road. She grinned and grabbed for Rebecca's arm.

"Oh my God!" she squealed. "Come on, I swear I'll show you how to do this one."

Beau's attention was drawn back to the table.

Rebecca's eyes went wide, a silent plea for Tara not to put her through that kind of torture. There wasn't much time before the band got to the first beats.

"I'll help you, too," Daniel assured as he offered his hand out to Rebecca.

That was probably the only reason she stood from the table at all.

"You coming?" Tara asked Beau as Daniel and Rebecca went to join the rows that were gradually forming on the dancefloor.

Anxiety fluttered in her stomach as they locked eyes and she mutely pleaded for him to take her invitation. This was the moment she had been waiting for and Beau couldn't turn her down, not after the way he had appraised her earlier in the parking lot. These cutoffs had to push him over the edge.

Beau cracked a smile and gave a nod. "All right. But if I trip over my boots, it'll be your fault."

Without another word, she grabbed for his hand and they came to stand in the same line as Daniel and Rebecca. With Beau on her left and her best friend on her right, Tara knew she had to make this moment count. Rebecca needed to wow the pants right off Daniel if Tara ever hoped to get a moment alone with Beau. And judging by the way they seemed to cling to one another already, she was pretty confident it wouldn't take much work.

There were just about a thousand variations to this dance, and some of the guests behind them were already in the middle of those complicated kicks, turns, and stomps that went above and beyond what Rebecca could master in one sitting.

So Tara, as well as the boys, kept it at her level. In time with the music, Tara showed her the four basic heel kicks, the two front hitches, and the stomp when it was time to turn. Rebecca was just about as uncoordinated as Tara had expected, but she started to get the hang of it.

As soon as she did, she abandoned her friend to Daniel's occasional guidance and turned to Beau. All while she tried to give Rebecca instructions, he had been doing extra spins, so he could face her without stepping out of beat.

"And you were worried about tripping over your feet!" she shouted over the band, a massive grin splitting her face.

Beau winked and she just about melted.

There was something about being in a line dance with a couple dozen other people that made Tara feel a little more alive. Maybe it was in the way everyone moved in synch, having a blast as they shared a communal dance to their favorite song. When Tara was dancing, she loved it all. She didn't really understand why she had quit it in high school. Possibly because it was all for competitions or showcases for school assemblies. There was a forced element in the way she had to learn the steps and attend practices.

Here, she was free to step off the floor and take a break, or keep going with the rest of them. And everyone else wanted to be there too, which made everyone enjoy it that much more. Except Rebecca.

Tara was too busy laughing at the faces Beau made at her and the extra sly moves he threw in to notice that her friend was struggling a bit.

It was only when Rebecca let out a soft cry that Tara came to a stop. Luckily, the other dancers were spaced far enough away that she wouldn't stop the flow. Daniel supported her as Rebecca seemed to be favoring her right ankle.

They all ushered her off the dance floor and sat her down back at their table.

"I think she twisted her ankle in one of the stomps," Daniel said.

Rebecca waved him off as he knelt down to

test her ankle's flexibility. "You don't have to do that, really."

Tara wondered if her friend really was hurting or if she just wanted to get off the dance floor. When Rebecca looked to her with no hint of pain in her expression, it was confirmed. The extra nudge of her head toward Beau who was just as focused on Rebecca's foot as Daniel was, Tara understood her perfectly and tried to suppress her smile.

"I don't think it's broken," Daniel reported, "but I've got some bandages in my truck. It'll keep the joint from moving too much."

Rebecca placed her hand on his shoulder. "I'm so sorry to have ruined your fun," she said, feigning her guilt.

Daniel lit up at her touch. "Not at all. I'm just sorry you got hurt."

With that, he helped her to her feet and escorted her out of the bar, leaving Tara and Beau standing next to their table. They were alone now and the stars must have aligned, because the band decided to slow things down with a good ole' fashioned two-step.

Tara bit her lips together nervously, hoping against all odds that Beau would ask her to dance so Rebecca's fake injury would not be in vain. She saw that Beau neither sat down, nor eased in to make his move. If she had drank anymore earlier, she might have taken this bull by the horns and dragged him onto the dance floor herself.

"So," he said, "do you wanna – "

Tara spun, a bit of her hair flying about her shoulders. "Yes!"

What she didn't see was that Beau had his hand extended toward the table. Her smile faltered when she realized what he was truly asking.

"Oh, sorry," she tried to recover. "I thought you were going to..."

Somehow, even bringing up the opportunity for an intimate couples dance was so much harder than trying to convince him to join a line dance. This held more personal meaning. She would have been inviting him to hold her close and sway to the music, maybe even have a private conversation as the other couples who were wrapped up in their own little worlds.

Beau's outstretched hand came to rub at the back of his neck as if he were just as embarrassed as her. "If you want to dance, we can dance too. I just wasn't sure if you were a little wore out from earlier."

Did she look tired? Was she sweating? Oh God, what if she was sweating and her deodorant wasn't doing its job.

"No, I'm not tired at all," she said. "But if you don't want to dance, I understand."

Suddenly, Tara felt like they were back in high school, both of them awkward teens who didn't know how to ask for what they really wanted. This shouldn't have been so hard.

Beau took a breath and let it out, along with whatever burden he seemed to be carrying. "No, I want to dance with you." He offered out his hand to her and she gladly took it, her smile returning.

When they took their place on the floor, joining in with the other couples who were steadily two-stepping in front of the stage, Tara swore up and down that she was in heaven. With Beau holding her, their bodies inching closer and closer as the song progressed, she had never felt happier. All the anxiety she had felt earlier was gone, frightened away by his warm blue eyes.

Each time she looked up into his handsome face, she felt that familiar tingling in the pit of her stomach and that ache that centered even lower and refused to go away. Why did he have to be so damn sexy and attractive?

"You know, I used to have a crush on you," he suddenly said in a hushed tone so only they could hear.

Tara tried not to giggle when she replied, "Really?"

Beau nodded without the slightest hint of remorse. "I did. But I know you didn't even notice me."

What a slap in the face after he just caressed it with such an admittance. She winced at the confession, knowing it was completely true.

"And I'm sorry for that."

Beau shrugged. "It's in the past. We were just kids, right?"

Tara wished it could have been so easy to blame her ignorance on her youth, but it wasn't completely that. If Beau had walked into the coffee shop, whether he looked like the guy on the cover or not, she would have noticed him only because he was hot. If he was as plain, thin, and gangly as he was in high school, she might not have given him a second glance.

Beau was a great guy on the inside, but she would have never known it if she hadn't been drawn to his outward appearance first. Suddenly, she felt unerringly guilty for being so petty and shallow.

She would have broken off the dance right there if Beau wasn't still holding her close. He knew the truth, and he didn't seem to care. Or maybe he did all along, but he was trying to give her the benefit of the doubt. He was giving her this second chance to find out what a great catch he was and Tara had to grab it with both hands or she might lose him forever.

"Do you forgive me?" she whispered, staring up into his eyes as tears burned at the corners of her own.

Beau's chest rose and fell with the great sigh he heaved. After a moment of deliberation, he nodded. "I do."

And Tara had to believe him. She had to believe that he was willing to give it a shot with this obvious connection they shared. Every look, every touch, everything screamed that they should be together. Book or no book, their destinies had to be intertwined somehow.

The song hit a few last notes and faded, but Tara didn't want this to be the end.

Without thinking, without reason or under the influence of anything but Beau's intoxicating spirit, she stood up on her tiptoes and planted a long kiss on his lips. He went rigid at first, but then melted into it, his grip tightening around her shoulders as their chests were pressed together.

Her fingers gripped the edge of his shirt sleeve, a wordless plea for him to hold her in that kiss for the rest of eternity. Or at least until closing time. The taste of his lips was sweeter than anything she had ever known. A current of pure bliss streaked through her body. It started in all the places he touched her and kept going straight down to where she needed his love.

She heard a few whoops from the other bar goers and Beau was the first to break away. By the burning look in his crystalline blue eyes, Tara knew that he felt the same. Her parted lips begged for more, but Beau took a step away, taking his warmth and support with him.

She nearly stumbled, but caught herself in time to stand on her own two feet. He kept a firm hold of her hands, but Beau must have seen the wisdom in keeping some distance from her. Tara almost agreed with him. It may have been wrong to kiss him like that, so quickly and without really knowing where they stood, but she couldn't resist it anymore.

Beau looked toward the door, then back to her as a slight flicker of panic alighted his gaze. She looked to see Daniel had come back inside without Rebecca. The look on his face expressed enough and Tara understood the gravity of her error.

There must have been a reason Beau was holding back and this had to be it. Daniel was the one to ask her out in the first place. Even if he was giving Rebecca more attention, Tara was who he had preferred from the beginning. Beau had tried to be respectful and give his brother chances to move in, and she didn't even see that.

So many thoughts came barreling in, confusing her further. What if Beau really didn't want to dance? What if he didn't forgive her for ignoring him in high school? What if he still liked her, but he had gotten over her after all these years?

Tara felt a rush of heat to her face and it spread across her shoulders until she thought she wouldn't be able to breathe under this new wave of anxiety. What had she done?

She left Beau on the dancefloor and ran straight past Daniel to leave the bar. Rebecca was sitting in the passenger seat of her car, her ankle wrapped up and shoe in hand.

"What happened?" she asked quickly as Tara pulled out her keys. Running away might not have been the greatest solution, but it was the best one she could come up with for now. She needed time to think and read the next chapter of that book. Maybe it would give her some direction on how to fix the mess she had just made.

"Tara!"

She turned to see Beau hustling across the parking lot, but she didn't want to hear any half-hearted apologies or explanations. She just needed to get home.

Angling into the driver's seat, she cranked up the engine and waited for Rebecca to close her door before speeding out of the parking lot. Luckily, she swerved in time to miss the two brothers who had come running after their dates.

"What the hell is going on?" Rebecca demanded.

Tears brimming at the corners of her eyes, she shook her head. "I kissed Beau."

"That's great!" she cried. "Why aren't you back there making out with him?"

She gripped the steering wheel more tightly as she slammed her foot down on the accelerator. "Because I'm an idiot and I shouldn't have kissed him. Daniel was my date and Beau was trying to be all respectful of that, and I just ruined it."

A stretch of silence passed between them before Rebecca broke it. "Daniel saw you kiss him?"

Tara nodded, feeling her throat close up with all the crazy, unwarranted emotions that would soon choke her.

"Damn," she muttered. "I told him to go in and tell you that I wanted to go home. Maybe if I had stalled a little longer – "

"No," Tara interrupted. "It was my fault. I don't even know what to do now. I like Beau so much, but he wants me for his brother, I know it. He doesn't want me." She didn't need the book to understand that much.

Her friend had no consoling words, no sage advice to give. All she did was reach out and touch Tara's shoulders that were already shuddering with the impending sobs.

CHAPTER SIX

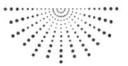

DIXIE'S SCHOOL WOULD LET OUT IN ABOUT thirty minutes, but there was some place Beau needed to go first. None of them had heard from Tara since that night at County Line Bar. Not a single text, call, or message anywhere. He had sent her a friend request on Facebook, but she hadn't accepted it yet, which could have meant anything. Either she didn't see it, or she denied him. He crossed his fingers for the former, but after the way she ran out on them, it was most likely the latter.

He parked his truck in front of the dentist office and tried to silence his thundering heartbeat. If he had any other reason for popping in, then this might not have seemed as awkward and uncomfortable as it really was. He didn't need to make an appointment, not for himself or for Dixie. He was there exclusively to see Tara and he tried to tell himself that it was simply to find out if she was all right and if they could somehow redeem this insane situation they found themselves in.

Deep down, he needed to make sure she was all right instead. Ever since that night, he couldn't stop thinking about her. He constantly checked his social media and his messages, hoping that she would reach out. But there was only silence. Ringing, heart shattering silence. It was getting to the point that he couldn't even lasso a calf or set a brand straight, because his mind wouldn't shut the hell up.

He thought about her laugh, her smile, the way she looked with her hair dripping wet onto her shirt, how the taste of her lips drove him wild. He wondered what she could have been doing at every given moment. If she was having a good day at work. If she had gone back to the coffee shop where they met. If she dreamed about him in the same way that he dreamed about her.

For a while, he felt like he was going out of his mind. Dixie wasn't helping matters, because she was just as eager to see Tara again too.

Daniel, made him feel even worse. There was no explaining away what happened that night. His brother had been furious with him at first, flying out in a rage that Beau rarely ever saw him in. After he tried to explain that it was just a kiss and it was Tara who did the kissing and not Beau, Daniel wasn't pacified in the least. Their attachment was already hanging by a thread and that kiss was the razor that sliced up every last hope either of them had. Beau didn't know who to be more angry with, himself or Tara for ruining everything that could have been with Daniel.

His brother was given to a mild fit of despondency and hardly came up for air after he buried himself in office work. Between Beau spending extra time in the pastures to get his mind off Tara, and Daniel being so absorbed in his work to ease the pain of losing Tara, Dixie spent quite a bit of time by herself up at the house. She could take care of herself, but an eight year old could get into so much more mischief when she was unsupervised.

But Beau wasn't here to beg Tara to come up to the house to occupy Dixie. Tara was probably the last person Daniel wanted to see. He came so he could prove to himself that if he saw her one more time, it would be enough to end this maddening, vicious cycle of puppy love. His job and his sanity depended on it. If he could see her again and not lose his head, then he knew he could get over her again in the same way he got over her before. It'd just take a lot of time and a lot of groveling to get her to come back to the ranch.

He was almost relieved to see the lobby a little busy. It meant he would have more time to form what he would say. He didn't see her at the front desk and for a moment, he wondered if she was even working today. Rebecca was there, her long blonde hair pulled back, but she didn't seem to notice him yet. Standing behind the elderly man at the counter who was making an appointment to get some bridge work done, Beau craned his neck to peek toward the back of the office and into the file room. From what he could tell, she wasn't there either.

Then, he heard her laugh from down the hall leading to the examination rooms and he thought it was a good thing his hands were in his pockets. Otherwise, all the people waiting in the comfy armchairs might see the way they shook. He thought his heart had been hammering before; now it might have been throbbing right out of his chest.

He took a deep breath to calm himself. This was insane. He had ridden bulls, broken wild mustangs, and even wrestled a boar to the ground with his bare hands. No animal alive struck so much fear into his heart the way Tara did. He shifted his weight from one foot to the other and wondered if he should just turn around and walk back to his truck. Sending a text might have been less nerve-racking than this.

But before he could take a full turn, she came hurrying down the hall with a load of files in her arms and hair bouncing around her shoulders. He couldn't help but grin when he saw her, but as soon as their eyes met, her own smile wilted like a delicate flower in the harsh summer heat. The spark of fear in her eyes told him all he needed to know.

Somehow, he had hoped that maybe she just got busy or had other things going on in her life. That wasn't it at all. Tara had been avoiding them, just as he originally assumed. He never claimed to understand the female mind, but he couldn't understand why she ran away from the bar the way she did. Was it something in the way Daniel looked at them from across the dance floor? Was it because Beau had pulled away from her when she obviously wanted more? Was she embarrassed, because he didn't return her kiss the way she had expected?

Tara froze for a moment and she shifted as if she wasn't sure whether to turn and retreat into the back or go to her empty seat beside Rebecca.

Beau forced himself to look away and try not to be as confused as he was.

Tara did come back to the counter and set down the stack of files she had been carrying before walking around the dividing wall between the back area and the lobby. She came right up to him without provocation.

"I'm taking my lunch," she said over her shoulder to Rebecca. She looked up in mid-sentence and gave her coworker a startled look. Then, one glance toward Beau seemed to curtail whatever reprimand she was about to dish out and then waved her off. Did she understand what they were going through?

Tara leaned over the counter and snatched up her purse before walking with Beau toward the door. At least she saved him the trouble of asking her to leave with him for a while.

"I came to see how you were doing," he said once they were standing on the sidewalk.

Tara slipped her purse onto her shoulder and wouldn't lift her eyes from her feet. "I'm all right," she said at first. "Work's been busy and there's been a lot on my mind."

If Beau hadn't seen her first reaction to him in the lobby, he might have believed her. They looked pretty busy as it was, so it was no wonder that Rebecca looked a little miffed that she was taking an impromptu lunch. But what had she been thinking about? Had she been able to untangle this mess, unlike him?

"Dixie hasn't stopped asking about you and when you'll be coming over next." Beau had to make this seem like it wasn't about them. He had to gently ease into that topic. "I think she got spoiled."

Tara's smile returned and she nodded. "I had wondered if she would."

Beau took a step closer and he saw her stiffen. "I was hoping you'd call. I didn't want to bother you if you weren't up for company, but I just wanted to make sure you were all right."

The torn expression in her eyes made him second guess his previous assumption. Maybe she hadn't made sense of it all yet. Beau knew exactly how he felt, knew exactly what he wanted. He just couldn't have it and his devotion to his family prohibited him from expressing how he truly felt. He thought just one dance, one tiny confession wouldn't be such a big deal. But it had been, and maybe that's what confused her now. He hadn't stuck to his convictions and that's what got them in this mess.

Tara picked at the skin around her nails and didn't answer for a while. "Can we talk somewhere else? It's kind of chilly out here."

Beau looked across the street to the coffee shop and bookstore where they had met and offered it to her. She agreed.

The barrister, Rachel, gave them both a furtive, sly look and fixed their beverages of choice, along with a sandwich for each. It wasn't until they took a seat at one of the round tables near the corner that Tara even bothered to look at him again.

The table was barely big enough to hold both sets of legs underneath and Beau had to be careful not to brush her ankles or knees with his own.

"I didn't call, because I needed time to think," she finally said in a hushed tone that was barely audible above the soft jazz music playing over the speakers.

"About that night at the bar?" he asked, trying his best to keep his voice even and low.

Tara seemed to struggle with the words, then took a breath and let them fall out. "I know you were trying to hook me up with your brother."

Beau hadn't been physically slapped in the face, but he certainly felt wounded all the same. By the bold, but scared look in her eye, he knew there was no point denying it. He thought when Daniel asked her out that would be enough to convince her that he didn't have a hand in the affair at all. What gave it away? "Did Daniel say something?"

"No, not exactly." Her gaze fell to the space between them.

"Did Dixie say something?"

She shook her head and a thin lock of hair danced beside her cheek. "No, it was nothing anyone said, it's just... I just have an intuition about some things... And I just kind of put the pieces together, you know?"

He couldn't accept that. There was something deeper than just her instinct or intuition. Something in his mannerisms must have set her off, though he couldn't think of a single instance where he would have given her that impression. He had always tried to make it about everyone else but him. Dixie needed a mother, and Daniel needed a new wife. It was that clean-cut, that simple, but it had gotten so out of hand.

He let a slow breath leak out between his lips and ran his hands through his hair. "You have to understand where I'm coming from on this."

Tara lifted her chin. "That's what I've been thinking about. I do understand. Dixie needs a mom, the ranch needs a bookkeeper, and your brother needs a wife..." Her eyes scrunched just the tiniest bit, in that way that made him think she was about to burst into tears. "But, I can't be any of that. I don't know what you were thinking, or why you thought playing this game was – "

"This was never a game," he interjected. "This was about taking care of my family."

As soon as he said it, Beau wished he could have taken it back. The fear in Tara's eyes turned into pure rage. He sympathized with her completely.

"Do you realize how misleading this has all been?" she hissed. "If you really cared, you should have told me from the beginning. We shouldn't have danced and I shouldn't have kissed you. If I had known what this was all about, I wouldn't have even thought for a moment that this was about us."

"Would you have gone to the carnival if I came out and said everything up front?" He didn't wait for her to answer. "No, you wouldn't have. And I didn't lie to you. It was about Dixie and I made that clear in this very café when we met."

"I kept reminding myself that you just wanted a playmate for Dixie, nothing else. And then you had to go and..." She looked away and he could see the slight quiver in the way she pinched her lips together to try and hold back the words. It didn't work. "There were so many little things that made me want to believe differently."

Damn, Beau wanted to hate himself for ever coming to see her. He should have just left well enough alone.

"You know what?" he said, throwing up his hands in surrender. "Fine. I get it. I screwed up. Maybe I pushed too hard, or I dropped too many hints, I don't know what I did. But just do me this one favor and don't punish Dixie for my mistake. Don't do this to her."

Tara's mouth hung open. "I haven't done anything except kiss you and sabotage your perfect little plan to hook me up with your brother. This has nothing to do with Dixie."

Nothing to do with Dixie? Now he was mad. "You may never want to date my brother, or work on the ranch." Beau made a valiant effort to keep his voice down. "But whatever you do, don't just drop Dixie like this. I know we got our wires crossed, but it doesn't change my resolve on anything. You don't even have to come by the ranch. I'll drop her off at your apartment if you really don't want to have anything to do with me or my brother."

"I never said I didn't want to come to the ranch again," she contested. "I never said I didn't want to see you or Daniel again. All I said was that I needed to think things over...

You really messed me up that night talking about how you had a crush on me and everything."

Messed her up? If only she knew what a disaster he had been since she left that night from the bar. If only she knew how desperate he was to learn what she really thought of him. Did Tara hate him? Love him? Did they feel the same or were they far from being on the same page? Hell, were they in different libraries entirely?

Rachel cut in just as a tiny tear slid down Tara's cheek. "Here you go," she said, setting down a tray that was much too big for their table. She distributed their drinks and their sandwiches, but even after Rachel left, neither of them touched their orders.

Beau nodded. "I get it. Really, I do. I'm sorry for not being up front about this. If I had been honest with you from the beginning, this wouldn't have gotten out of hand." He reached for his coffee cup and absent mindedly twisted it. Right now, he had no appetite for coffee. He just wanted to hop back in his truck and forget the whole thing.

Tara didn't move for a while, neither of them even touched their food. "I'll come up and see Dixie this weekend, if you think that's all right."

Beau looked up to her and saw the utter brokenness in her eyes. He never wanted to see her so sad, never wanted to see her so upset. But at least she was seeing it from his side now. He knew he had no chance with her now. He had deceived her and Daniel from the beginning and now he was paying for it. She probably didn't even want to be with Daniel at this point. Neither brother could have her, not any time soon anyway. "I think that'll be fine."

He thought he saw her lips try to pull into a faint smile as she nodded. "Thank you for understanding... I hope we can still be friends, even after all of this."

Friends. Damn it, he didn't want to be friends. He wanted to be so much more. He wanted to open up and tell her everything, how much he enjoyed that kiss, how he had wanted to be with her for so many years. He wanted to confess everything, but for the sake of the small glimmer of a chance that Tara could fall for Daniel in the distant future, he had to keep his mouth shut.

Unable to speak for fear that his broken heart would start putting words in his mouth, he only nodded.

"I'm really sorry for the way I behaved. I really am."

Beau's phone trilled in his pocket and he

quickly fished it out. "Dixie just texted me," he told her. "I've got to go pick her up from school." He hadn't been so keen when he heard that Daniel gave the kid a phone, but it certainly came in handy. Saved by the eight-year-old.

Tara gasped and started to wrap up her sandwich. "I'm sorry," she said again with a bit of sniffle. "I probably kept you here way too long."

"It's all right. Don't leave on my account," he said as he stood from the table and accidentally bumped her knee. Even that little touch tempted him to stay.

"Oh, it's fine," she replied quickly with a flustered wave of her hand. "I've got to get back to work before Rebecca has a cow. We've been busy all morning."

Even though he was running behind, he waited for her to hurriedly gather up her lunch and latte. She slid out of her chair and in the process, knocked her purse over. The contents, mostly makeup and little things like a notepad and her phone, spilled out onto the tile floor.

Tara cussed under her breath and stooped down to gather everything up with trembling hands. "I'm so clumsy," she groaned.

Beau laughed and, if it were appropriate, he would have told her that he would never consider her to be clumsy. Not after the way she danced circles around everyone that night at the bar.

He squatted to help scoop up the pens and bits of used straw wrappers that tumbled out. Underneath the table, he saw a book, front cover faced down on the tile, but he wasn't sure if it had been there before they sat down. They were in the bookstore, after all. Someone could have left it.

Before he had a chance to reach for it and ask if it was hers, Tara stood and shouldered her bag. "I'm really sorry for ghosting on you guys, but we're all good now, right?"

Beau stood as she snatched up her drink and sandwich. "Yeah... Yeah, we're good." That was a total lie, but they didn't have time to go into that right now. "I'll let Dixie know you're coming over this weekend... Listen," he said, reaching out to gently place his hand under her elbow. "I am sorry for what I did... or tried to do. I didn't mean to put you in an awkward situation, believe me."

Tara gave him a forced smile. "I didn't mean to either, I swear... Let's just forget the whole thing. This is for Dixie, right? Then let's just let it be about Dixie and keep going from there."

Agreeing with her nearly broke his heart,

but he nodded and dropped his hand before he was tempted to pull her close and try something stupid – again.

Tara turned and rushed out the door, leaving Beau at the table with his coffee and sandwich. He stooped down to retrieve the book he had spotted earlier. Rachel was probably missing it, or would need to shelve it again, so a customer could buy it.

When he dusted off the cover, he was shocked to see a familiar face staring back at him.

What the hell?

Beau slowly sat in the chair and stared at the male model on the cover, who looked surprisingly like himself. The girl in the back was familiar too and he instantly picked it up as a likeness to Tara.

He read the back description and then the first few pages, though his phone vibrated with a few more text notifications from Dixie. This was insane. Did Tara write this? Checking the publication year, that theory was impossible.

Yet, how could a story follow so closely to what had happened last week when they met? Almost nothing seemed different except for the names. Even the town was so much like Brooksdale and a bar just like County Line.

It was only when Dixie finally called that

Beau was able to pull himself out of his stupor and hurry to his truck. He'd have to read more when he got back to the ranch. At least he managed to do two things. He had procured a playdate for Dixie for the weekend and managed to shatter any hope he had with Tara. Maybe now he could empty his head of her.

IN THE COURSE of the afternoon, Tara completely forgot about the sandwich she had stuffed in her purse upon leaving the coffee shop. She didn't have an appetite in the least. Just when she thought she was over the disaster that had sent her spiraling into a dark hole of emotion that she could barely crawl out of. Nights spent in a fit of tears, she almost didn't want to pick up that stupid book.

But she forced herself to. The moment she came home that night from the bar, she read as much as it would allow. The next two chapters had magically appeared and she finally got her wish.

It was from the hero's perspective.

Beau's perspective.

But what she read had sent her reeling harder and faster than that kiss they shared at the bar.

Tracy wasn't his and wouldn't be, if everything went right. David deserved the girl this time.

From what she gathered, David was the fictional counterpart to Daniel.

Tara nearly dropped the book, her hands were shaking so badly. What did he mean by not his and never would be? Daniel – David – wasn't the sexy cowboy on the cover. Beau was. This obviously wasn't Daniel's romance, because Beau's point of view was finally presented. It was what she had feared as soon as she locked eyes with Daniel the moment she pulled away from Beau's kiss.

Tara's heart beat hard against her chest until she was sure it would burst. She wasn't even sure she was breathing as her eyes poured over the words. With every sentence, she ventured deeper and deeper into the heart of the man she thought she understood, the man she thought she had come to love.

Beau never intended for her to be his girlfriend, even though it was clear that he wanted her to be. Not even close. From the very beginning, she knew it was going to end this way, but she still let herself sink neck-deep into this crazy dream. This couldn't have been what the book intended. If this wasn't her romance, then what the hell was it? Just some magical, mystic prank?

Everything they did had always been centered on Dixie and Daniel. The carnival, the horseback riding, the card playing, dinner, all of it. None of it had been about her and Beau or what kind of relationship they could have together. She was getting matched up with Daniel, who might have really felt something for her too. Why would Beau want to do that when the book stated so plainly that he was attracted to her? Then, the harsh reminder of what happened to Daniel's wife came crashing back to the present.

Tara was no replacement for Dixie's mom, and she certainly didn't want to be the rebound for Daniel. What was Beau thinking? He couldn't just screw with people's lives like this. He made her believe that he wanted her.

No, scratch that. The book made her think that he wanted her. In all reality, if she had never found this book or read about this alternate reality where her name was Trish and his name was Ben, then she wouldn't have gotten so excited about becoming the heroine to his hero.

The tears wanted to come, but she forced them back. She wouldn't be one of those silly girls who pined away in unrequited love for a guy that wasn't going to give her the time of day. She didn't want to get angry at Beau for practically using her either. It wasn't his fault that she was nearly falling apart. He never really made his intentions known, but he never led her on either. Not really. It was all in her head.

Beau was the dedicated brother and uncle that she believed him to be. That had never changed since the moment they met. Even after they kissed, he denied his true feelings for her.

That's why she had to think. Tara didn't know whether to continue to pursue him, despite everything she had learned from the book, or keep her distance for the sake of the fragile balance between heart and duty.

Tara didn't want to be with Daniel, and as much as she loved Dixie, she could never be what Beau intended. And perhaps ghosting on them would ease the pain of the moment she had to crush their hopes. That didn't happen.

For days afterward, she tried to sever all thoughts and ties with the family. As soon as the book ceased to fill in the blanks for her, she set it aside in her purse and tried to forget it. But just as if she were expecting some message, she continually checked it for another update, another hint that things might be mended between them.

Seeing Beau standing there in the lobby might have unraveled everything she had worked so hard to hold together. And leaving him now was just as hard.

Thankfully, Rebecca asked no questions when she came back into the office and dived right back into her work in an attempt to distract herself from the heartache.

CHAPTER SEVEN

Beau sunk deeper into the sectional cushion, the book clutched between his hands as he continued to read through the first half of the novel. Ever since he had gotten home from picking Dixie up, he'd become engrossed in this story about Tracy and Ben. It didn't take him long to realize it was really about Beau and Tara. He didn't know how this book could exist, but for the moment, he didn't care. He needed answers.

With Daniel still wrapped up in his work and Dixie outside playing with the dogs, Beau had a couple of hours to learn exactly where Tara was coming from.

Since the very beginning, she had been clueless about it all. Against everything he had tried to imply, she really believed that they were going to end up together. He read about the joy she felt when he paid her any bit of kindness and the tears that streamed down her face as she drove home from the bar. He even read about the arousing moments when she was in the shower and when he held her tight on the dance floor. Whoever this preternatural author was, they were immensely talented in making him feel for the twisted plight of the characters.

When he came to the chapter where he and Tara had their final meeting in the café, Beau turned the page to find it blank. He flipped back and forth, ahead a few pages, and then thumbed through the last quarter of the book. Nothing.

He made a sound of disbelief which gained the notice of his brother down the hall.

"You all right?" he hollered.

Beau hardly knew. He thought the kiss at the bar was instigated under the influence of alcohol, but to learn that Tara was completely in her right mind and eager to kiss him since the moment they met, it changed everything.

"Yeah, I'm fine," he called back, then snapped the book closed to stare at the cover in amazement.

All this time, she wanted him just as badly as he wanted her. He saw the furtive looks and returned the witty banter, because he needed to at least be friendly. But it turned out that Tara didn't want Daniel in the least and she chided herself so harshly for never noticing Beau before.

It made him understand her reaction at the bar, why she distanced herself from the Bremors over the last week or so. He had been so blind and overly gallant that he had never stopped to really think how she felt through this whole ordeal.

Now he knew. And now had to make things right.

He tossed the book on the adjacent cushion and went to Daniel's office. Even if Tara couldn't be his wife, the man still needed a bookkeeper. Stacks of papers, receipts, and manifests covered his desk to the point that he couldn't see a bit of clear space whatsoever.

Daniel looked up from his keyboard and his fingers went still. "What's up?" he asked, probably seeing his brother's bemused expression.

"Tell me something straight," he began, hoping that without the book's guidance, he could somehow begin to wrap up this mystery. "Tara... Do you even like her?"

He eased back in his office chair and laced his fingers over his stomach. "You know, I thought I did... She's cute and you may not like her long legs, but that's definitely one of her more redeeming features."

Beau leaned his shoulder against the doorframe and crossed his arms. "I hear a 'but' somewhere in there."

Daniel made a face as if he were wrestling with the words. "Like I said, she's great. But her friend..." He whistled. "Rebecca's pretty hot."

There was no way he would agree. Tara could probably roll out of bed, no makeup, her hair a mess, and she'd still outshine every girl in Texas. "So you like Rebecca?"

Daniel's eyes narrowed. "Why are you so interested in who I like all of the sudden?"

That's when Beau knew he had to come clean. He told Daniel all about his master plan to get him and Tara together, how that had been his goal from the start and how it had back fired the other night at the bar.

His older brother listened. The flames of despair and rage that had shined so bright in his eyes last week were gone now. Apparently he'd had time to think over things too.

When Beau was finished pouring out his confession, Daniel didn't say a thing at first. They just stared, brother regarding brother and the only noise came from the barking dogs and giggling girl outside near the barn.

"And you like Tara, don't you?" he asked, a faint smile gracing his stone cold face.

Beau nodded. "I think I love her."

It was a bold proclamation. Beau had never claimed to love any woman in his life. But he knew that if this fire he felt for Tara hadn't fully died away after spending so many years apart, it must have been love that he felt.

It wasn't just a fleeting notion or a passing fancy. It wasn't just a high school crush. This was pure, true, undying, unconditional love. Why else would he forgive her for ignoring him in school and going MIA on them after she left the bar? Why else would he feel this unending ache for her touch, to hear her voice, and see her pretty face? Why else would his heart still be holding on after all they had been through – after all he had put them through.

Daniel smiled. "Then you can have her with my blessing."

Beau rolled his eyes and turned away. As if he even needed Daniel's blessing. Knowing that he wasn't even interested in Tara was blessing enough.

Before he left the office, Daniel said, "And one more thing. Don't try and play match-maker again. You suck at it and I don't need my little brother to hook up dates for me. When I'm ready, I'll take care of it."

He nodded and realized that's probably what he should have been told from the beginning. He was a damn fool from the start. Hopefully Tara would take him back, even if he had to get down on his knees.

TARA TORE off her bed sheets, though she knew it would have been absolutely silly to think the book was tucked against her mattress like that. But she was running out of options. Her tiny, one-bedroom apartment had been turned upside down in order to find that missing novel and the panic steadily began to build in her chest.

When she had gotten back to the office after meeting with Beau, she had wanted to check the book to see if anymore had been written. It was way too addictive not to check, even if her heart had crumbled into a thousand little pieces. She knew it hadn't fallen out at the café, but she went there right after work anyway to see if Rachel might have found it under the table where she and Beau had been sitting. No one had turned in a book to her.

So thinking she'd just left it at home on her nightstand, she hurried back to her apartment. It wasn't there either. Tara had been searching for over an hour now, but the book was absolutely nowhere in her apartment.

She wasn't so much worried that she had lost the book. Too many hours had been wasted fretting over what would appear in the magical pages next to make her realize this wasn't healthy. She couldn't just wait around for words to appear on a page and dictate her life. The book wasn't something that could determine her fate. She had to do that herself.

What she was more worried about was someone else finding the book and reading what was in there. Yet, if it fell into the hands of another reader, would the story change? Would the cover change? Or would they read this crazy, mixed up story about her and Beau? Would they make the connection that she was really Tracy and Beau was really Ben?

Tara dropped to the foot of the bed and ran her fingers through her slightly disheveled, tangled hair, as she leaned against the edge of the mattress. She hadn't taken that book anywhere besides work and home, and she had already asked if Rebecca had seen it anywhere. She hadn't. Somehow, she figured that she wouldn't even need to ask. If Rebecca found the novel and saw Beau on the cover, she would have made a huge deal about it already. She wasn't the type to play anything cool.

She sat and held a moment of silence for the lost book. It was certainly fun and entertaining while it lasted. Now, she only had her own memories to remind her of the amazing times she'd had with Beau and his family. And now was her chance to make her own path, decide her own actions when it came to Beau and Daniel.

Who knows, maybe now that they were past this awkwardness, she could actually pursue Beau like she wanted. He seemed to have given up on his mission to set her up with his brother, now that she knew the whole truth. Maybe they could start over, just like they'd agreed in the café?

She pulled out her phone from her back pocket and opened her Facebook app. She had ignored his friend request for too long. With a shaky finger, she tapped the accept button and let out a long breath.

A knock came at her door and she nearly jumped out of her skin. She hadn't even heard any footsteps. These walls were paper thin so it was impossible not to hear her neighbors trouncing down the halls at all hours of the day or night.

She looked around her apartment, to the tossed throw pillows on the floor by the sofa, and the way the pots and pans had been pulled out from the kitchen cabinets. It looked like a tornado had hit the place, but with luck, whoever was at the door wouldn't stay for long. Maybe one of her neighbors had heard her tearing up the apartment and wanted to make sure she wasn't being robbed.

Tara opened the door and looked up into a pair of stunning, troubled blue eyes. She nearly crumbled.

"What are you doing here?" she asked, unable to slide that filter in place between her brain and her mouth.

Beau smiled and held up her book. Her stomach did several backflips and she was sure she'd puke right there on his shoes. "It said you lived at the Magnolia apartment complex, second floor, third door down the hall on the right... And here you are." He gave a small laugh and looked down at the cover. "I'll be honest, I wasn't quite sure if you'd be here or not."

Tara's heartbeat pounded in her throat and she wasn't even sure if she could speak clearly. Somehow, the words managed to find a life of their own and poured out. "You read it? All of it?"

He nodded. "As much as it would let me... Can we talk?"

Glancing over her shoulder to the chaotic

mess, she seriously didn't want this to be his first impression of her apartment. Though, if he had read what was written so far, then he already knew what her apartment was like. Would he know about this mess? Did the book predict that for him?

She swung open the door and let him inside. He let out a whistle just as she shut the door. "I think the book understated this."

Tara crossed her arms over her roiling stomach. "I lost it."

"And you were looking for it," he interrupted. "I know."

Then, he kindly offered her the book. She took it and pressed it against her chest, hoping that it would calm everything with its mystic juju, or whatever it was that made the words appear on the page.

"So you know everything now," she stated, unwilling to meet his gaze that felt hot on her skin.

"Not everything," he said, his voice dropping an octave. "Where did you find that book?"

Tara took a deep breath and leaned against the wall by the front door. "In Rachel's bookstore. I pulled it down, because I liked the cover, but I didn't realize what it could do until you walked in."

His brows shot up. "You found it the day we met?"

She nodded. "And when it started to show everything that was happening, I knew I had to keep it."

"And that's how you found out about my idea to set you up with Daniel?"

She nodded again. "I read about it the night I came home after we left the bar."

Silence stretched between them and Tara didn't know whether to ask him to sit on the sofa, with its cushions thrown over the coffee table, or offer him a drink, since the glasses were already pulled down from the cabinets.

Instead, she did what she had been itching to do for half the day. She opened the book and flipped to the page where she thought she'd left off. Sure enough, their meeting that morning was written there, plainly from his point of view. She skimmed over it and he slightly let her, probably already knowing what she was looking for.

She came to the part where it read that Ben's heart was shattered when she spoke. It said that he had wanted nothing more than to be with her since the moment they'd met, but now there wasn't a snowball's chance in hell that they could, since she had lost almost all her faith in him. That just wasn't true.

Tara closed the book and risked a look up to Beau, who seemed just as nervous as she was. He had no reason to be nervous. He should have known, after reading the first part of the story, that she was head-over-heels for him.

"I never meant to hurt you," she said.

"And I never meant to hurt you, either."

Tara gulped and offered up the book. "Does it say what's going to happen next, or will you tell me?"

Beau took a few cautious steps forward, but she refused to move. No more running, no more denying. They both wanted each other; they knew it, and there should have been nothing left for them to figure out.

He wrapped his strong arm around her waist and pulled her in for their second kiss. Tara closed her eyes and dropped the book, so she could properly wrap her arms around his neck. Her fingers weaved into his hair and he did the same. She loved the way he kissed. So smooth, tender, and filled with a quiet passion that she could definitely get used to.

At their feet, the book began to dematerialize and vanished, but she didn't even notice. She was far too busy paying attention to where his hands roamed across her hips and waist.

Beau pinned her to the wall by the door, making the sheetrock shiver with the force of it.

If her neighbors didn't think anything was going on in her apartment before, they certainly would now.

As if passion had taken the wheel, Tara found herself hitching on of her long legs around Beau's thigh, pull him in until she could feel his hardness behind the zipper on his jeans. They moaned together and Beau kissed down Tara's jaw until he came to her slender neck. Each nip from his teeth and caress of his tongue along her skin sent out amazing currents of pleasure that skittered through her limbs until she was trembling for more.

"Are they expecting you back tonight?" she asked breathlessly as her eyes rolled into the back of her head.

"Nope," he mumbled against her neck. The vibration of his deep voice added to everything else she felt and Tara moaned again.

It was a good thing they weren't expecting him back, because Tara was positive that he wouldn't leave this apartment until the following morning.

She tugged at the hem of his shirt, demanding its removal. Beau broke away just long enough to strip them both of their shirts. The feel of his skin on hers was magnificent, warm, and so sensuous. She could feel the edges of his ripped abs and sculpted muscles glide across her stomach as he rocked into her. The only thing in the way were their jeans, but they'd soon take care of that.

One of Beau's hands found their way to her bra and cupped one of her breasts trapped beneath the soft padding of silk. Her nipple hardened and Tara moaned a little louder as he gently massaged her breast in his palm.

She leaned the back of her head against the wall, arching her back to wordlessly implore him to go further. He released her chest and hoisted her up off the ground, forcing her to wrap her other leg around his waist.

Somewhere in the haze of foreplay, Beau pulled her off the wall and carried her into her bedroom, which was just as much a disaster area as the rest of her apartment. If she had known that Beau would be coming over and that any of this would happen, she wouldn't have yanked the sheets off and thrown them in a pile on the floor beside the bed.

He dropped her down and Tara bounced against the mattress. Before she knew it, Beau had his hands on her pants and was pulling them off.

A sobering thought entered her mind and Tara bolted upright. "Condom," was all she could say.

As if predicting her panic, he slipped one

out from his back pants pocket and presented it to her. Tara grabbed for it, but he snatched it out of reach.

"Not yet," he purred before dropping down to suspend himself over her. "Too soon for that."

Tara claimed his mouth in a demanding kiss, slipping her tongue in without another thought. Sweeter than honeysuckle and her mom's special blend of sweet tea, Tara could have become addicted to him. Why had she waited so long? Why did they waste so much time dancing around their feelings? They could have been doing this a week ago and it still might have been long overdue. In fact, it had been overdue since high school.

Beau's hand slid behind her and unclipped her bra before tossing it to the floor. With her breasts freed, she could feel the radiating heat of his skin on hers. The taut nipples pressed into his chest, tantalizing them so effectively that she wondered if she'd come right then.

This was insane on so many levels, but at the same time, it felt so right. Everything from the way his hands slid down her sides, sending chills through her core, to the way his mouth seized her nipples to suckle them, it was all so right and perfect.

With each flick of his tongue on her nipple

and raking of his trimmed nails across her skin, Tara could feel herself drawing closer and closer to her climax. But it wasn't fair. He was about to make her explode with mind-blowing foreplay and he still had his pants on.

His fingers hooked on the edge of her lacy panties and she was sure she heard a light ripping sound as he pulled them down to dangle from one of her ankles. Naked, but not completely. Before Beau could come down on her again, Tara pushed herself up and grabbed for his pants.

"These are in my way," she said, a playful smile dancing across her lips.

Beau returned the smile and didn't protest as she worked at his belt buckle and boxers. It shouldn't have surprised her when she laid eyes upon his thick, slightly moistened cock. What surprised her more was how much she lusted after it. Before she could take that for herself as well, Beau dropped to his knees, denying her the pleasure of taking him the way he was about to take her.

His mouth trailed along the inside of her thighs first. With his hands under her knees, and pulled until half of her body was hanging off the bed. He pushed her legs apart to receive him and Tara couldn't help but watch the way his mouth captured her folds.

But that didn't last long. Tara threw her head back as a fresh wave of mounting pleasure tightened her core until she thought she couldn't hold it in anymore. But hold it she did. Because she wanted this to last.

Just as his tongue had toyed with her nipples, so did it tease her clit and slip in to lap up the moisture that practically dripped from her. Her fingers had nothing to grip as she continued to moan and cry out for release.

Who knew that Beau could be so powerful, and yet so tender in lovemaking?

When the moment came, her breath hitched and she whimpered even louder as the pressure reached its breaking point. She came and Beau was there to taste the fruits of his labor. Her back arched as the orgasm crested, leaving her body racked with little spasms as he continued to torment her with more flicks of his tongue and grazing of his lips along her tender, throbbing skin.

Tara closed her eyes and was only vaguely aware of Beau tearing open the condom package. She hastily tried to recover so she could do the honors herself, but she was far too weak to move much less return the favor he had bestowed to her.

She had never known such world-spinning,

amazing sex could exist, but here Beau was, proving her wrong once more.

He scooted her back onto the mattress, grabbed her by the ass as his leverage. She could feel the head of his cock play between the folds, gliding up and down to tease her further. Tara's body responded in kind and she hooked her legs around him as more heat pulled between them.

It shouldn't have been possible that she wanted another, not after experiencing the best orgasm she had ever had. But when he played with her breasts again, gearing her up for another round, she almost couldn't contain herself.

Her body received him, slow at first. Beau only ventured in a little bit, but it was enough to make her gasp and dig her nails into his broad shoulders. She tried to rock against him to force him inside, but he resisted her.

"Slow," he whispered, as if that was supposed to make her want it any less.

Tara groaned in protest. "Now."

Beau eased in further, filling the core of her desire until Tara shuddered in ecstasy. With aching slowness, he pulled out and pushed back in, thrusting into her with climbing urgency. Tara held him close, savoring this feeling for as long as her body would allow.

It was hard just to think straight as he pounded into her, his face buried into her neck as they moaned and gasped with every thrust. Tara felt her whole universe spin out of focus and the only thing that existed in perfect clarity was Beau and her feelings for him. There was no way the book could have predicted this because no mind on earth could fully comprehend the kind of utter bliss she experienced when they came together as one.

She could feel her climax coming a second time and she wasn't too shy to let Beau know through her screams. He pumped faster until they orgasmed in unison. Intertwined, they spiral down from their erotic high.

Tara shuddered and felt the aftershocks course through her nerves as his cock pulsated within her. They sighed together and rolled to the side. It was a wonder he had any strength at all to pull her up onto the bed, so they could lay beside one another.

A light sheen of sweat dotted her forehead as she tried to catch her breath. Sex took the wind out of her even more than line dancing.

Beau's arm encircled her waist, a gentle reminder that he was still there and still completely real. He wasn't some fictional character from one of her books that left her as soon as she slipped it back on her shelf. He wasn't going to disappear again like he did after graduation. And she sure as hell wasn't going to ignore him anymore.

He had a good soul and a tender heart. The body, the arresting blue eyes, it was all icing to sweeten this already yummy dessert she had been gifted. She reached out to stroke the stubble on his cheek. With his face half-buried in the pillow at the head of her bed, he opened his free eye and smiled to her.

"Why couldn't I have found you sooner?" she wondered aloud.

Beau reached up and took her hand in his to kiss the back of her fingers. "Doesn't matter," he replied. "I'm here now."

Tara edged closer. "You were always there and I never saw it. I know I -"

He wouldn't let her continue and captured her mouth in a silencing kiss. Apparently he didn't want to hear all of her regrets and her apologies. She had so much to atone for, so much she felt like she had to make right by him. One evening of outstanding sex wasn't going to do it.

She grabbed him and pulled him closer, deepening their kiss until he finally pulled away to speak.

"I love you," he whispered. "I always have." So out of the blue, but so right for the moment.

Tara could only grin. "I love you too. And I always will."

Maybe she didn't have to make up for so much. If he loved her anyway, she didn't need to prove her newfound devotion to earn back his trust. And with just a few simple words, she made her own declaration that she'd want to spend a lifetime getting to know him and catching up on all their lost time.

AFTERWORD

ABOUT THE AUTHOR

A paranormal author of eclectic tastes, Sheritta Bitikofer has a passion for storytelling. Her goal with each book is to rebel against shallow intimacy and inspire courage through the power of love and soulful passion. Her biggest thrill comes when she presents love in a genuine light, where the protagonists not only feel a physical attraction to one another, but a deep emotional (and dare we say spiritual?) connection that fuels their relationship forward into something that will endure much longer than the last pages of their novel. A devoted wife and fur-mama to two shelter rescue dogs, Sheritta's life is never dull. When she's not writing her next novel, she can be found binge-watching her favorite shows on Netflix, eating chili cheese fries, singing and dancing to a wide

genre of music, or painting at a medieval reen-
actment event.

Follow her for upcoming novel releases
www.moonstruckwriting.wordpress.com

The Decimus Trilogy

The Beast of Verona

Amber Ashes

Saving the Beast